AF347866

So grateful for the amazing reviews and kind words about my first book, House #872!

"Congrats Madhav! Best wishes for the success of your book!"
-Legendary **Kapil Dev**,
First World Cup Winning Captain,
Former Cricketer

"Excited to read your book. Congrats Madhav!"
-**David A. Steinberg**, Co-Founder,
Chairman and CEO, Zeta Global

"Amazing! You are truly a Renaissance Man! Can't wait to see what you do next."
-**Steven Gerber**, President,
and Chief Operating Officer, Zeta Global

"Wow!! This is amazing!! Congratulations! I am so happy for you. Such an accomplishment!"
-**Denise Lang**, Senior Vice President,
Legal and Deputy General Counsel, Zeta Global

"Madhav has a fine eye for detail and a very compelling narrative style."
-**Asit Baran Pati**, India's leading F&O trader

"I like the beautifully free flowing style of your writing. It is absolutely effortless and natural. Looking forward to more titles!"
-**K.K. Krishna Kumar**, Former President BGVS and Asst
Director (Retd), State Institute of Languages (Kerala)

"Really loved the narration. Amazing work! Wishing you all the best!"
-**Narain**, Indian Film Actor

"Weaves together so many lives, deep friendship & experiences while addressing contemporary issues in a very light read... cover to cover in one sitting... very well written... waiting for the next instalment…all the best!"

-Biju K.K., Vice President,
Fidelity Center for Applied Technology, Boston

"Just finished reading House #872! It's an awesome page turner. Couldn't keep it down before getting to the last page. Cheers to many more books penned by you!"

-Bimal Nair, Senior Manager,
Amazon Web Services, Dallas

"Super! House #872 is rocking! So proud of you dear!"

-Nandini Das, Assistant Manager, Union Bank, Cochin

"Wow! Amazing!"

-Krishna Das, Software Professional, Cochin

"Sometimes a book can outdo a great film! The charm of this book is such that you get engrossed in the lives of the characters. The writing is eloquent, honest, and simple. It feels intimate and warm. Impressed by Madhav's work! Keep it up!"

-Neetu Prabhakar, Mrs. India International

"It's amazing to see the success of your book! You have gone global! Congratulations!"

-Sandra Santilli, Chief People Officer,
TMRW Life Sciences, New York

"After a long time, I read a book which refreshed my old memories. Nostalgic! Great narration!

-Faruk Shaik, Managing Director (India), Zeta Global

"A superb book where I could feel I was remembering my college days. The book is extremely intelligent of the age depicted. Every person has their own effect. It is light, diverting, sensational and enthusiastic. A must read!"
—**Priyanka Sarkar**, HR Professional, Mumbai

"This is an amazing feat Maddy! So happy and proud of you!"
—**Deepak Bhuvneshwari Uniyal**, Co-Founder, Insurance Samadhan, and Shark Tank Participant

"Outstanding! Heartfelt congratulations!"
—**Gurucharan Singh Gandhi**, Author of 'Kabeer in Korporates' and 'Echoes of Gasping Souls'

"Congratulations Madhav! All the best!"
—**Patricia Nolan**, Senior HR Leader, Wolters Kluwer, Philadelphia

"Super articulation…Your book took me to the old memory lanes…"
—**Ranjan Raje**, Assistant Vice President, Deutsche Bank, New Delhi

"Thoroughly entertaining. It is fast paced and does not waver from the storyline unnecessarily. A fun book about friends and friendship. Takes you to college days. Really loved it."
—**Divya Madhav**, Hyderabad

"Amazing book! Congrats!"
—**Sophie Vaes**, HR Business Partner, Zeta Global, Belgium

"Wow! Congrats Madhav! Did not have any idea that you would be writing a book!"
—**Veronika Pleskova**, Legal Professional, Czech Republic

"Great work! Many congratulations, Madhav! Keep going!"
-**Harish Krishnesh**, PepsiCo, United Kingdom

"The plot is quite captivating and different from any usual college life I've heard of. Four people from different corners of the country, their aspirations, struggles in their journey and them building their own future is interesting to read. Hoping for more of your astounding works…"
-**Farina Francis**, College student, Bangalore

"I personally believe Madhav has immense potential that is waiting to be discovered further. House #872 is a good start to his writing journey and I'm confident of more to be written by him."
-**Siddharth Jain**, Industrialist, New Delhi

"The author has treated the narration in a simple and beautiful way. When you read the book, you know its straight from the author's heart. A tale of friendship and growing together in it."
-**Manju Narain**, Singer and Actor, Chennai

"Amazing story! It will hook you like an interesting web series!"
-**Sudeep Sharma**, Head – HR, HCL Healthcare, New Delhi

"Super! On my reading list for the summer. Congrats Madhav once again!"
-**Corinne Saunders**, Managing Director (EMEA), Lionbridge

"Finished reading…awesome…waiting for the next one!"
-**Smitha Ramesh**, Dubai

"Wow! This is so amazing! You are such an inspiration…...Congrats Madhav!"
-**Avinash Kohli**, Ex HR Leader, Boeing, Singapore

"Congratulations!! Such a proud moment for you to have become an author now!!"

-**Aanchal Dhawan**, People Strategist at Publicis Sapient, Germany

"It is a testament of time-tested friendship withstanding."

-**Jo Yaneza**, Payroll Associate at Zeta Global, New York

"Congrats Madhav! Great to hear about your book!!"

-**Jaswinder Singh Brar**, Australia

"This is fantastic! Congratulations!!"

-**Stephanie D'sa**, Vice President - Strategic Consulting, Zeta Global, London

SECOND INNINGS

Madhav Das

ZORBA BOOKS

ZORBA BOOKS

Published by Zorba Books, February 2023
Website: www.zorbabooks.com
Email: info@zorbabooks.com

Title: **Second Innings**
Author Name: Madhav Das
Copyright © Madhav Das
Printbook ISBN :- 978-93-95217-41-5
Ebook ISBN :- 978-93-95217-40-8

Zorba Books Pvt. Ltd. (opc)
Sushant Arcade,
Next to Courtyard Marriot,
Sushant Lok 1, Gurgaon – 122009, India

Printed in India

To

My Mother

About the Author

Madhav Das grew up in Ras Al Khaimah (in United Arab Emirates) and Pattambi, a small town in Kerala. After his graduation from Government College in Pattambi, he went to Delhi to do MBA. He stayed in Delhi for 15 years and then moved to Hyderabad.

He has spent close to two decades in the corporate world in HR leadership roles devising, executing talent strategy, and leading teams across India for several multinational companies. He is currently the Senior Director – HR in a global marketing technology company headquartered in New York. He has won several national awards for leadership and HR Excellence. He is also a social media influencer and speaker at various leadership conferences and B-schools across India.

He finds time for writing during the weekends. House #872, his first book is a bestseller with readers in more than 20 countries. House #872 received endorsements and great reviews from celebrities and readers across the globe. Second Innings is his second book.

Madhav lives in Hyderabad with his wife Divya and children, Avantika, and Avinash.

To know more about Madhav, visit www.madhavdas.com or email him at dasmadhav@gmail.com. To connect with him, log on to Facebook at www.facebook.com/madhav.das.16, Instagram at www.instagram.com/madhavdas210, or tweet to @MadhavD210

This book is a work of fiction. The characters, places and incidents described in this book are either the product of the author's imagination or are used fictitiously.

The opinions expressed in this book do not purport to reflect the views of the Publisher.

Acknowledgements

Thanks to God for the love and blessings. I am forever grateful to you for this life.

Thanks to the Universe for conspiring in a way that this book sees the light of the day.

Thanks to Dr. Wayne Dyer, Oprah Winfrey, Steve Harvey, Dr. Joe Dispenza and Esther Hicks for teaching me the power of gratitude and appreciation. Thanks to YouTube for taking me to the amazing sessions of these great people.

I'm grateful for the blessings of my father (Late) K.M. Haridas and my mother Meera Haridas. I'm forever indebted to them.

Thanks to my wife Divya Madhav, and my children Avantika and Avinash for their love and support.

Thanks to my uncle K. K. Krishna Kumar, my sister Nandini Das, my brother-in-law Krishna Das, my nephew Advay Krishna. My in-laws Rajagopal.P and Premalatha Rajagopal, my brother-in-law Deepak Parambath and his daughter Dhriti Deepak. Thanks for the love and support. Thank you all for being there.

Thanks to all the members of my extended family for the love and appreciation always.

Thanks to Asit Baran Pati, my bestie, and the central character of my first book House #872.

Thanks to Mandeep Anand for being a great pillar of support.

Thanks to Chetan Bhagat for being an inspiration.

Thanks to Legendary Kapil Dev, Hon. Judge Sudheer Kumar Mummineni and Mrs. India International Neetu Prabhakar for their kind words and endorsements.

Thanks to all the readers and well-wishers for making my first book a great success! I'm so grateful for your love and encouragement to keep writing more books.

Thanks to Team Zorba for ensuring global reach for my books through various online bookstores.

Special thanks to my better half Divya Madhav and my friend P.V. Priya - the first readers and editors for their exceptional efforts in editing the manuscript.

Thanks to Sithesh for the brilliant cover designs of House #872 and Second Innings.

Thanks to my social media followers, including those on Facebook, LinkedIn, Twitter, and Instagram. I am thankful to all of you.

Thanks to the editorial team at Zorba for their inputs. Their guidance and support are invaluable.

With that, I welcome you to Second Innings!

Madhav Das

List of Characters

1. **Puneet Khosla** – *Founder of a SAAS startup which gets listed on NASDAQ*
2. **Rajesh Khosla** – *Puneet's father and Sales Director in an Insurance company*
3. **Ruchita Khosla** – *Puneet's mother*
4. **Rina Khosla** – *Puneet's sister and Jewelry designer of global repute*
5. **Trisha Swaminathan** – *Puneet's wife*
6. **Karthik Swaminathan** – *Trisha's brother and Puneet's batchmate*
7. **Nilanjan Basu** – *Rina's husband and IAF officer*
8. **Abhinav Basu** – *Nilanjan and Rina's son, cricketer*
9. **Anirban Basu** – *Nilanjan's father and investor in Puneet's company; Managing Director of one of the business units at Kwoley*
10. **Srabani Basu** – *Nilanjan's mother*
11. **Neeta Bhatia** – *Ruchita's sister*
12. **Aditya Bhatia** – *Neeta's husband*
13. **Rahul Bhatia** – *Aditya and Neeta's son and Puneet's business partner*
14. **Mike Kohler** – *Rahul Bhatia's friend and investor in Puneet's company*

15. **Sarah Wilson** – *Mike's ex-girlfriend*
16. **James Kohler** – *Mike's father and a successful realtor*
17. **Linda Nolan** – *Rahul and Mike's boss during their internship*
18. **Vinay Gulati** – *Rajesh's colleague*
19. **Ekta Gulati** – *Vinay's daughter and Mike's wife, VP- Product Development in Puneet's company*
20. **Amardeep Singh Lamba** – *Rajesh's boss*
21. **Romil Singh** – *Deputy Chief Minister, Delhi*
22. **Nidhi Sharma** – *Romil's wife*
23. **Philip Winslet** – *A Chef based in London, Rina's boyfriend*
24. **Howard Smith and Anurag Saxena** – *Mike's business partners and Puneet's friends*
25. **Caroline Garnier** – *Rina's boss in Paris*
26. **Neetu Sharma** – *Rina's senior from college and her first boss*
27. **Jenny Smith** – *CEO for Asia Pacific at Kwoley*
28. **Manish Sahai** – Kwoley *India CEO and Anirban's boss*
29. **Harpreet Kaur** – *Kwoley India CEO's Executive Assistant*
30. **Kulwant Singh** – *Anirban's colleague and Sales Director in Kwoley*
31. **Ravinder Kumar** – *Office support staff member in Kwoley, starts an NGO later*
32. **Shreya Bansal** – *Puneet's batchmate and his partner in the NGO*
33. **Sunil Tandon** – *Nilanjan's senior*

1
San Francisco

It was Mike's second week as an intern in Facebook. Facebook's headquarters in Menlo Park sits on the edge of San Francisco Bay, on a sprawling campus that feels more like a town than an office. "MPK," as insiders call it, covers more than 250 acres and contains more than 30 buildings.

More than half of Facebook's global employees work out of Menlo Park, and this massive team does "a little bit of everything." People specializing in engineering, product, communications, and virtual reality are all scattered randomly across the campus.

Mike's best friend, Rahul Bhatia was with him. Both joined as interns in the Communications team.

"Amazing campus! I have heard that they hired consultants who helped design Disneyland to build out the main street of this campus," Mike said.

The main street looked like the fusion of Palo Alto, the nearby town where Facebook was founded, and Downtown Disney.

Rahul smiled and said, "They have got everything here. Philz Coffee, a barbershop, and an outpost of Sol."

Sol is a Palo Alto based Mexican Restaurant. Facebook's founders loved Sol so much, they convinced the owners to open an outlet in the campus.

Both were amazed to see the sculptural metallic creations, the open-plan buildings with big windows, well integrated into the surrounding ecosystem.

"The architects have done a great job! So mindful that they have kept fritted windows, which keep birds from crashing into the glass," Mike said.

Rahul nodded. As they moved ahead, they noticed some fox safety signs posted outdoor, warning visitors to keep their distance. "We're Cute, Famous and WILD!!!" the sign explained.

They had to meet Linda Nolan, their new boss. They reached the cafeteria. Linda was waiting for them. She greeted them very warmly and took them inside the cafeteria.

The buffet spread was so impressive. They started with some chicken pozole, a traditional Mexican soup. Mike and Linda were big fans of Indian food, so they decided to go for tandoori chicken, paneer curry, and garlic naan. Rahul went for some Mexican stuff as he liked the soup very much. Linda explained to them about the projects lined up and some of the immediate expectations from them. She shared the details about the other stakeholders involved in the project. The meeting really helped Rahul and Mike gain some quick insights into items which are critical to success.

Linda's cousin worked in Mike's father, James Kohler's real estate company.

James Kohler is a very successful realtor, and his company owned lot of luxury homes in Florida. Their gated Orlando neighborhood featured golf homes, luxury lakefront condos and lakefront estates in a breathtaking setting. Spanning 500 acres of rolling hills and crisp, cool lakes, it is one of the most recognized private gated communities in Florida offering unparalleled style of living.

2
New Delhi – 10 years back

Rajesh Khosla was so happy about his promotion. He knew that he was the most eligible person in the Zone for the Sales Director role.

He called his wife Ruchita to share the good news.

He said, "Hey honey! Finally, I got the letter. The much-awaited letter."

Ruchita responded, "Wow! Congratulations Mr. Sales Director! So proud of you!"

He said thanks and passed on the sweetest kiss to her on phone. They also discussed that they would go to Vaishno Devi for Mata's darshan and on the way back to Golden Temple in Amritsar. Ruchita makes it a point to visit Golden Temple once a year.

Rajesh was given 20 new offices to manage in addition to the 10 offices he was responsible for earlier as Regional Manager of the Zone. Those 20 offices were in Punjab, Haryana, Himachal Pradesh, and Jammu & Kashmir (J&K).

He told Ruchita, "I'm bit apprehensive about J&K but it is also a good opportunity to create a turnaround story."

He was very bullish about Punjab and Haryana as he knew the offices in both these states were doing so well and there was scope to generate more sales there.

Ruchita knew that he had passed on couple of leads to his Punjab counterparts in last 2-3 years and they made good fortune out of it in terms of the incentives. She sincerely believed that if you do good karma, it will come back to you in due course. This promotion, she believed was part of that karmic plan. She was so happy for him.

Rajesh's first official visit was to Panipat in Haryana. Vinay Gulati is the Regional Manager for Haryana, and he was supposed to accompany Rajesh.

Vinay had almost 15 years of experience in the insurance sector. He had worked for almost 4-5 insurance companies and considered himself to be a walking dictionary of insurance!

He rarely listened to anyone. His subordinates when called for a meeting would walk into his cabin knowing they will be muted for next few hours! They had to be on a listening mode. Otherwise, they would be blasted by Vinay for all the sales opportunities they missed since their birth!

Vinay and Rajesh stayed in South Delhi.

As they had to reach Panipat by 9 am for the meeting with the office head and sales managers, they decided to start from Delhi around 7 am. Vinay was the first one to board the cab and he went to Rajesh's house to pick him. Vinay was bit nervous as he has heard that Rajesh sets very high standards for performance and is very goal oriented. He is one leader who may not be just happy seeing the efforts put in. He needs real numbers and could give tough time to those who don't deliver sales numbers consistently.

He reached Rajesh's house. He called on his mobile.

Rajesh answered the phone in just one ring. He said "Hi Vinay, have you reached? Just give me 2 mins."

Vinay responded, "Ok Sir"

Ruchita did a daily ritual of perfecting Rajesh's tie knot before he leaves for office. She did it as usual. Rajesh kissed her and moved towards the gate.

Vinay was waiting in the car. As soon as the gate opened, their driver went towards Rajesh to pick his bag and placed it in the car after folding the back seat. Rajesh had specifically asked Vinay to get the Innova so that they can have a very comfortable trip.

Vinay greeted Rajesh, "Good morning, Sir. How are you?"

Rajesh responded, "Good morning, Vinay. I'm good. So nice to meet you. I've heard great things about you."

Vinay had a happy face. He wasn't expecting those kind words from Rajesh as his region did not do well in the previous quarter.

Rajesh asked, "How was the kickoff meet?"

Vinay responded, "It was great! We had around 100 sales managers and close to 300 agents participating in it. "

"That's fantastic!" Rajesh exclaimed.

He continued. "Are they excited about the new sales incentive plan? We had to really fight for it with the Distribution Head. Hope there will be more people qualifying for Executive Council (EC) this time."

Vinay answered, "Yes, they are very excited. We will have at least 15 people qualifying for the EC and at least 7 or 8 sure shot MDRTs. Just keeping my fingers crossed!"

Executive Council is a recognition platform for encouraging agent advisors in NYC Life Insurance Company to get them qualified for MDRT.

Million Dollar Round Table (MDRT) is a global, independent

association of the world's leading life insurance and financial services professionals from more than 500 companies in 70 nations and territories.

Making it to MDRT is nothing less than winning a Nobel Prize for the insurance folks!

Rajesh has heard from Vinay's ex-boss that he is not very process centric. Also, he has not really grown in the companies he worked. He always made it to the next level by switching companies. As they say, rolling stones gather no moss!

But Rajesh did not want his preconceived notions to cloud the working relationship with him. He always believed starting on a clean slate. He has tasted success in turning around lot of laggards and took pride in it.

Both kept talking, reviewing the sales strategies and talent upgrade plans for the office in the region. Within 2 hours, they reached Panipat.

Tarun Baweja, the office head of Panipat and his staff were waiting to receive the new Sales Director and the Regional Manager. They had put up some floral decorations and had arranged for bouquets. The receptionist welcomed Rajesh and Vinay with the bouquets. Tarun and his team clapped welcoming their bosses from Delhi.

Rajesh smiled and commented, "Thanks guys. So nice to meet you all. But don't make it a practice to get bouquets every time as I will be visiting my offices very frequently."

Vinay looked at Tarun and smiled. That smile conveyed a lot to Tarun.

Tarun was hearing such a comment from a senior official for the first time. Normally, they cherish such hospitality. But he understood that Rajesh is a very candid and cost-conscious leader.

Soon Rajesh and Vinay did a 'meet and greet' with the team and moved into the conference room for some meetings to discuss the agent recruitment target and sales pipeline for the quarter.

3

New Delhi and San Francisco

It was Ruchita's sister's birthday. Neeta is Ruchita's youngest sister. She is very fond of Ruchita, and their bond got stronger when they stayed together in Delhi for some years. Neeta studied in Delhi College of Engineering (DCE) and Ruchita had welcomed her with open arms along with owning up her education expenses. Their parents are from a small town near Ludhiana. Neeta moved to San Francisco after working in a software company in Bangalore for few years.

Ruchita waited till 7 pm IST to call her sister and wish her happy birthday. Neeta normally wakes up by 5:30 am her time.

Ruchita dialed her number, but she got a voicemail response. She thought Neeta might be sleeping so didn't try again.

After half an hour, she got a call from Neeta.

"Hi Didi, Sorry I missed your call." Neeta said

Ruchita said, "Happy birthday Choti. So rahe the kya?"

Neeta responded, "Thanks a ton, Didi. As always, you are the first one to wish me!"

Ruchita smiled and asked, "So what is the plan for today? Has Adi returned from Chicago?"

"Yes Didi. He came back yesterday. We are planning to visit Napa this weekend for the birthday celebration. We thought of going ahead with Rahul's recommendation this time."

Neeta's son, Rahul always preferred to go to places where he can appreciate nature and be at peace. He is so fond of painting, and he takes out time during the weekends to be out in nature and paint on the canvas.

Napa is a hot-bed of farm-to-table food and sun-drenched vineyards. Napa's wine country is a favored getaway for the fog weary. Neeta and family planned to visit Castello di Amorosa; an authentically styled 13th century Tuscan castle winery built by a fourth-generation wine maker to honor his Italian heritage!

Rahul told his parents that Castello di Amorosa is considered an architectural masterpiece with all elements of an authentic medieval castle. It took more than 8000 tons of hand chiseled local stone and nearly one million antique bricks imported from Europe to complete the castle.

Neeta said, "Wow! It might have taken many years for them to build it. Right?"

Rahul responded, "Yes, the construction took almost 15 years."

He did lot of research about the place reading reviews and then he convinced his parents that it would be a memorable weekend getaway.

Rajesh and Ruchita's son Puneet and their daughter Rina were also very fond of Neeta, their Mausi. She always made it a point to get extravagant gifts from the US for them.

Puneet was more into cricket (partly because of his father's pressure) and Rahul did not understand much of cricket as he grew up in the US. But they had a common interest in philately. They had stamps from more than 100 countries and always did a barter when they met. They also made it a point to visit their ancestral home in Ludhiana and spent good time with their grandparents.

Puneet went for cricket coaching to DC Cricket Academy in Delhi. DC Academy was the most sought-after academy for all the aspiring youngsters where they honed their skills under the direct supervision of some of the well-known coaches. The head coach in DC Cricket Academy had the distinction of training lot of international and national players.

Rajesh was so passionate about cricket but could not pursue it at an early age due to financial pressures and had to take up a sales job when he turned 18. He had to financially support his mother and 2 sisters. He had to go through lot of hardships very early in life and had to forget about his passion for cricket. Rajesh felt that through Puneet he will realize his long-cherished dream. Puneet was not very keen initially to take up cricket but his father's passion and the inspiring stories about lot of cricketers in Delhi motivated him to try his luck there.

4
New Delhi

Puneet's sister, Rina wanted to be a fashion designer and always imagined of having an impressive clientele. All her friends always admired her creativity.

Once her Physics teacher spoke in the class about Albert Einstein. While talking about his great contributions to Physics, she also spoke about how much Einstein believed in the Law of Attraction. She read out one of Einstein's famous quotes in the class – "Everything is energy and that's all there is to it. Match the frequency of the reality you want, and you cannot help but get that reality. It can be no other way. This is not philosophy. This is physics."

This quote had a profound influence on Rina. She tried it in small little ways, and it always came true. So, physics brought her close to the concept of Law of Attraction! She believed that whatever she thinks of becoming in future can come true if she directs her thoughts in that way and visualize it. That's how she got into the specifics of having a clientele.

She did not speak much about these things to others. Occasionally, she penned down some thoughts in her diary. She also felt that many people would not be able to relate to these things. She shared about her dreams and aspirations with her parents, and they only had one condition that she should secure good marks in 10th and 12th so that the onward journey becomes smooth. They were very strict on the academic side with Rina but gave Puneet lot of freedom as they felt he would take up cricket seriously and will have a successful career.

Rajesh did not want to give any other option to Puneet, as making him a cricketer was his most cherished dream!

The coaches in the Cricket Academy also realized this matter. After seeing Rajesh play once, a coach commented, "If you received proper training early in life, there was a high chance of you landing up in the national team."

He responded, "But destiny always have different things in store, and you need to just go with the flow sometimes and see where life takes you."

Rajesh always felt that he is extremely fortunate that he made a very successful career in Life Insurance rising to the position of a Sales Director, he could take good care of his mom till her last breath, he took care of all his responsibilities towards his sisters, and they are all well settled. He has a loving wife and two adorable children. He always felt that God has been kind and it is good that he had to go through lot of hardships very early in life so that he can proudly say to his children that he is a self-made man. He will always be an inspiration to them.

Rajesh had a great year with lot of Sales Managers qualifying in his region for the Annual R&R on criteria's like Annualized First Year Premium (AFYP), Number of Policies (NOP), Agent Recruitment etc. He also had 5 agent advisors qualifying for MDRT from the region and it was a big deal.

After 3 months, the entire team of qualifiers and the senior leadership team of NYC Life Insurance Company flew to Toronto.

The Million Dollar Round Table's (MDRT) Annual Meeting opened in Toronto.

The central theme of the meeting was "Changing Lives", chosen to represent the power MDRT members hold and how they can make a positive change in the lives of their clients. The meeting featured more than 85 speakers – including Olympic Gold Medalist Mary Lou Retton and Andes Mountain crash survivor Nando Parrado.

Rajesh was talking to Richard Davies, senior agent advisor from New York, and he came to know an interesting thing about the origin of MDRT.

Richard told him, "The name comes from a group of 32 successful life insurance agents who met in a hotel in Memphis, Tennessee. Each agent could demonstrate they had sold more than USD 1,000,000 of life insurance that year."

He continued, "That meeting took place in 1927 and it evolved into the formation of the organization that exists today – an organization dedicated to encouraging ethical values and sharing of ideas and concepts that have found to be valuable to establishing improved business practices."

5
Toronto

The conference was a big success, and everyone felt very inspired. Next 3 days was all about pampering oneself for all the hard work to get there at the first place. On the first day after the conference, the day trip began with the pickup from their hotel in Toronto. They boarded the bus to Niagara Falls. During the journey, they passed the scenic Niagara River and Lake Ontario.

Before reaching the waterfall, they stopped at the Whirlpool Spanish Aerocar. The next stop was at the Living Water Wayside Chapel. This chapel is a tiny white building snuggled neatly between two trees beside Walker's Country Market. It was built in 1964 by the Niagara Falls Christian Reformed Church. The chapel is famous for being the Guinness Book of World Records holder for the smallest chapel in the world. The NYC Life team considered it as a unique photo opportunity to stop by and see the World's smallest chapel and relax and enjoy a moment of spiritual reflection.

The day ended with a lavish buffet dinner at a hotel that directly overlooks the falls. The most amazing experience for all of them was the illuminating light show, marveling as fireworks and pyrotechnics transform the waterfall into a riot of color. The tour concluded with drop-off back at their Toronto hotel.

Next day, after having breakfast they boarded the bus to downtown Toronto – not very far from the hotel. After a 13-minute ferry ride, they reached Toronto Islands, also called the Toronto Island Park. This island is a group of 15 islands interconnected by pathways and bridges. The island is approximately 5 kilometers long from Ward's Island to Hanlon's Point.

Rajesh and his boss, Amardeep Singh Lamba wanted to be away from the sight of their team members, especially the agent advisors for few hours in the Toronto Island Park. It has been such a hectic schedule for them for last few days – helping their teams get the maximum out of the MDRT conference. The Niagara trip was full of pleasure but slightly hectic as they also had to take care of some team members who felt bit sick on the way.

Amardeep told him, "Such a nice sunny day with light breeze. Let us get some beer."

Rajesh responded, "Why not?"

They got Moosehead Lager. Amardeep is a beer connoisseur and had lot of knowledge about the beer brands across the world. Amardeep's villa in Gurugram housed a very lavish collection of single malt, wine, and beer. The high performers in the team always aspired to stay in that league as Amardeep invited a select few to his house every quarter. This was a big motivation for them in addition to all the cash rewards and recognitions the company offered.

He told Rajesh, "This is one of the best beers in Canada. They have been here since 1867. Moosehead Lager is brewed using 100% Canadian two-row pale malt and their unique lager yeast, then cool-fermented and cold-aged to achieve its flavor."

Rajesh took the first sip. The malt sweetness and hop bitterness in this golden, pleasant lager was perfectly equal. It was a refreshing taste, and he could instantly feel all the fatigue disappearing.

While talking to Amardeep, Rajesh saw a couple walking holding their hands and kissing. Very familiar faces! He just turned back to confirm whether they are from his team and to his surprise, he saw Romil Singh and Nidhi Sharma, the stars of their MDRT club! The most enviable love birds in the Island Park!

They were clicking selfies and enjoying each other's company. Amardeep also noticed them.

He asked Rajesh, "They are having a good time, eh?"

He continued, "Their bonding reminds me of my early days at Nestle. That was a blissful time!"

The beer was good enough to rekindle the sweet memories.

Rajesh responded, "Yes, the atmosphere is such and when you are in a foreign land, lot of inhibitions just fade away. I haven't seen them getting so close in Panipat."

Rajesh knew that Nidhi's father is a very successful realtor in Haryana. She was born with the silver spoon. Romil belonged to a family of politicians, and he is great grandson of former Union Home Minister and stalwart Ram Pratap Singh.

6

Toronto

Next day in the evening, Rajesh was on a video call with his family while walking in the lobby. He saw Romil and Nidhi coming out of the elevator. There was another person who walked out along with them. He had an odd smile on his face. Rajesh was amazed to see the full-blown PDA of Romil and Nidhi. He was seeing it for the first time.

He immediately dialed Vinay.

Rajesh said, "Hello. Sorry Vinay for bothering you so late. Just a quick one."

Vinay responded, "No problem, Sir. Hope you all are having a good time there."

Rajesh smiled and said, "Yes, some people are having a great time. Just called to mention about that."

Vinay exclaimed, "What happened, Sir?"

Rajesh said, "Romil and Nidhi are making it so evident to everyone that they are so thick in love. Amardeep was also asking me about them. I'm fine with the bonding and all but seems like they have forgotten that they are travelling with a group. I don't want unnecessary rumors later."

Vinay could sense it. He had specifically called Romil and Nidhi 2 days before their travel to give some friendly advice about the basic etiquettes as he knew that this couple has the capability of becoming Page 3 celebrities wherever they go.

Vinay had a very embarrassing moment 6 months back with them. This happened on a Saturday, when he and the trainer went to the training room to discuss something about the room setup. Both Romil and Nidhi were up to something, and they were so intense. It was very clear from their facial expression that they were interrupted.

The moment Vinay and the trainer walked in, Nidhi just pretended that she has headache and was behaving as if Romil was taking care of her. But Vinay observed the messy hair and the loosened buttons of her shirt.

After that embarrassing moment, Vinay walked out of the room and the trainer stayed back to discipline them. But everyone knew in the office that it was blind love, and they did not care about anything. They knew that doing sales numbers and winning awards is not a tough thing for them. They wanted a place where they can go daily for work and have some privacy as they could not venture out much in other places as they are from reputed families. That was the demerit of growing and living in a small town where everyone knew each other. Privacy is all what they needed, and they could barter anything for that!

Vinay did not want to share all this information with Rajesh.

He responded, "It might be due to the general vibe there. They know that it's very strict in the office."

Rajesh did not fully believe it. His only concern was about

Amardeep noticing it but at the end of the day, it did not matter. Only numbers mattered. But he did not want other team members making a big issue out of it. There were agent advisors from Chennai and Bangalore talking about Romil and Nidhi while having breakfast. Rajesh overheard them when he went to get some orange juice.

He said to Vinay, "Good night, buddy. Just wanted to inform you so that corrective actions are taken going forward. I have seen such relationships snowballing into big issues for us in the past, so I want you to be careful."

Vinay said, "Thanks Sir for letting me know. Will keep that in mind. You have a great day!"

Rajesh said bye and disconnected the call.

7
New Delhi

During the weekend, Ruchita, Puneet and Rina went to the Saibaba temple at Lodhi Road. After the darshan, they went to Eatopia in India Habitat Centre. Eatopia is their favourite family eating joint. It's a pocket friendly food court with separate counters for Indian street food, North Indian food, Chinese, Thai, Continental stuff and even pizzas and burgers. The delight is that one gets everything under the same roof. Even their pastries are so delicious. Ruchita wanted kids to have some fun as their father is away for more than a week now. She did not want them to complain to their dad that mom did not take them anywhere when he was away.

Puneet said, "Let's have raj kachori and pani puri first, then we will order some heavy stuff." He knows raj kachori is his mom's favourite snack. It's important to ensure the happiness of the host!

Rina nodded and said, "I want to have some chicken soup too."

Ruchita gave Puneet her debit card. He went to the street food counter and placed order for raj kachori and pani puri.

Then went to get soup for his sister.

Rina told Ruchita, "Dekho cricket practice se bahut fast hogaya apka beta. Pehle toh itna time lagta tha uthke jaane me!"

Ruchita replied, "Tum future national level player se kitna kaam karwa rahe ho?"

Rina laughed and said, "I want to train him well off field too!"

Puneet was looking at both and knew he would be the topic of discussion. Both mom and daughter are keen observers and will always crack some jokes out of anything that they observe.

Puneet placed everything on a tray and brought it to the table.

He asked his mom, "So what was the topic of discussion?"

Ruchita smiled with a wink.

Rina responded, "We were praising you for the athletic body language even while placing order for the food!"

Puneet said, "So funny!"

But he was happy to hear it. He was so glad to see his sister being appreciative.

After the initial round of snacking, they had chicken biryani, aloo paratha and some steamed momos. They also had Rina's favourite pineapple pastries.

They always felt a sense of contentment after having food at Eatopia. After paying the bill, they went for a walk inside the Habitat center campus. After a quick tour of a painting exhibition within the premises, they headed home.

When they reached home, Ruchita received a call from Rajesh. He was in the airport and wanted to inform her that boarding is about to begin. They spoke for few minutes.

She told him, "We are all waiting for you. Have a safe flight. Love you."

8
Modern School, New Delhi

Nilanjan Basu is the leader of the Bits N Bytes Technology Club in school. This club was founded many years back with the objective of spreading technology related awareness and knowledge among youngsters and adults. As the leader of this Club, he and his team participated in various symposiums and competitions organized by reputed institutions and consistently achieved laurels for their school.

Rina Khosla is the coordinator of the Fashion Technology Club. This club was formed with an objective to cultivate a passion for designing, illustration, and sewing skills. It encouraged member students to bring about the same brainstorming born creativity that they use as consumers to create a personalized and fabulous wardrobe or any creative stuff for themselves. Each year they hosted a fashion show where the students of 10th to 12th class enthusiastically designed things based on a particular theme.

Rina has always been a big fan of Nilanjan. His clarity, conviction and in-depth knowledge about many diverse topics amazed her. He was also the topper in the class. Rina was in the top three, but she could not make it to the first position for almost 3 years ever since Nilanjan joined her class.

Initially, she tried to be very competitive with him, then slowly she started witnessing a wave of admiration within her and she started falling in love with him. She loved the way he spoke.

Nilanjan also liked Rina.

After 6 months

One day in the school cafeteria, Nilanjan and Rina decided to reveal their true feelings for each other. They both felt like having that conversation many months back but somehow the situations were not right. As they say, there is always a right time for things to happen.

Rina felt something so magical about that afternoon. A heavenly feeling that makes everything in life better, brighter, and more beautiful. She has never felt any such thing for anyone in the past and she could feel a sense of security and comfort suddenly. A very different kind of feeling it was. She was extremely glad that Nilanjan also had the same kind of feelings for her.

She is a bold girl and always took lead in extracurricular activities. The most sought-after person to lead group activities and projects in the class. But suddenly she was feeling very shy in the class for the first time. She felt there is a new identity embracing her. Like childhood, the romance we choose to dub first love is swathed in a protective wrap of innocence and idealism.

Nilanjan also changed completely. He wanted to spend more time with Rina in the cafeteria and library.

They identified a quiet corner in the library and that corner became their favorite place within few days. Both felt that they had strong feelings for each other for quite some time and that might be the reason things fell in place so suddenly.

Nilanjan said to her, "I'm amazed to see how you have become the center of my world. It's a magical feeling!"

She smiled and said, "Time seems to pass by in split seconds when I'm with you."

Nilanjan saw a notebook in her hand.

He asked, "Is it a rough note?" Can I write something in it?"

She nodded with a smile.

He wrote, "There is no other space more soothing and surreal than with the love of your life"

She took the pen from him and drew some heart emojis around the line he wrote. The emojis were filled with red color using a sketch pen lying on the table. The Librarian was the first person to notice this unusual camaraderie between two frequent visitors.

Puneet also figured out after couple of weeks that Rina is in a different world. She did not have much time for the friends in their residential society. At home, she was not in her usual self.

On a weekend, she went with Nilanjan to PVR Priya. After hanging out in the nearby market for few hours, they went for a movie. That was the first date!

9
New Delhi - 4 years later

Puneet Khosla was bitten by the entrepreneurial bug as he was in the last semester of B Tech. His college created a learning-by-doing environment and designed some special programs for the self-motivated, independent thinkers.

Puneet and Karthik Swaminathan were best friends. They always had topics of common interest and bonded well right from the second year at college.

Puneet told Karthik, "We should really develop the skills to start our own business. It is always good to develop some foundational business skills along with the technical skills. What do you think?"

Karthik said, "That's a great idea! One doesn't have to be a jack of all trades. You can always get people with different set of skills onboard."

Puneet replied, "Yes, that is possible. But getting some idea about accounting, finance, marketing, and analysis will always help."

Karthik's twin sister Trisha Swaminathan was also in the same college, and she was widely regarded as the 'fashionista' in the campus.

Puneet had helped Trisha with an academic project which got her lot of accolades. His warmth, wit and intelligence turned her on. She appreciated intelligence to a degree that it actively stimulated her. She found Puneet to be a critical thinker with insatiable curiosity in life and knew that he will go a long way.

Karthik knew about his sister's infatuation towards his best buddy. He was fine with it as he knew Puneet will make it big in life.

Trisha once told Karthik, "I love Puneet so much. I may marry your best friend. What do you think?"

Karthik smiled and replied, "He is a great guy. He certainly deserves a better girl."

Trisha's face turned red and she started a pillow fight with her brother.

Karthik ran to the living room and Trisha ran behind with the pillow.

He said, "Ok, great idea! You should marry him. But does he love you?"

Trisha said, "I am going to find out very soon."

Karthik replied, "Yes, please keep me out of the loop. If you guys feel the same for each other, I will be the happiest person. He will always remain my best friend, whether he marries you or not."

Trisha picked up the pillow again. But Karthik picked his mobile and vanished.

10
Gurugram – 2 years later

Jenny Smith, the Regional CEO for Asia Pacific at Kwoley was trying to ignore the jet lag and focus on shopping. This was the first time she lost her baggage as there was some mess up during transit and she just had the laptop bag and a kit which had some essentials. She thanked her stars that she did not put that kit into the check-in baggage. Harpreet Kaur, Kwoley India CEO's Executive Assistant was with her in the Ambience Mall to help her with the shopping. Her boss, Manish Sahai was on phone checking with Harpreet if everything is fine. He did not want Jenny to get disappointed with anything.

Kwoley is a global leader in information services and practice management software for professionals and they had offices in 40 countries. Jenny Smith reported directly to the Global CEO.

Manish knew that the leaders of different business units and the staff are waiting for the townhall with Jenny, but the entire thing had to be postponed by 2-3 hours.

Jenny was happy that she could find almost all her favourite brands in Ambience mall. If it was a weekend, she would have shopped more but she was mindful about restricting it to essential buys. She was staying in The Leela so she could drop in at Ambience anytime. This is one thing she loved about staying in The Leela. Her India office is just few minutes away from the hotel and the biggest mall in the NCR region is just next door to her hotel.

Finally, she had a big smile for the anxious looking Harpreet after coming out of the mall. She looked very happy. She had changed into a business suit in the store itself as she had to conduct the townhall with the India team.

They both got into the BMW. Jenny called Manish and he picked up in one ring. Manish could make out that she is in good mood.

Manish Sahai called Anirban Basu, the MD of Tax and Accounting business into his cabin. Anirban was the blue-eyed boy of Jenny Smith. Jenny and Manish had a surprise announcement for the Tax and Accounting team.

"Jenny has received the approval to hire 20 sales professionals to launch P-Firm in India" Manish told Anirban.

Anirban responded, "Wow! That's great news!"

P-Firm is a very successful global product and is one of the most sought-after practice management software for Chartered Accountants. Anirban Basu and his Sales Director were the people behind the feasibility study for P-Firm in India. They felt that most of the reputed CA firms are looking for a product that can give them an edge over others and gain an early adopter advantage. P-Firm has to be made their first choice for the product in the market.

Anirban told Manish, "I'm very sure that this product will sell like a hot cake."

He had spoken to some of his counterparts in the US, Brazil and Australia to know more about the product and found it penetrated the market really well and did not have very credible competitors.

Jenny stepped into the office. Kalpana, the receptionist handed over the bouquet with a smile. Everyone expected that Jenny might not be in a good mood, but she was very jovial and made some observations about the facelift given to the front office. She shook hands with the staff and after a brief chit chat with them, she moved to Manish's cabin. The arrangement was done for the townhall, and everyone was waiting to listen to her address the gathering.

The townhall began. After Manish's introductory session welcoming everyone to the meeting, Jenny took over. Jenny could easily connect with the team. After an ice breaker, she shared about the important updates for the APAC region and some of the specific initiatives driven globally. Manish and Anirban were waiting for the most exciting news to be revealed.

She started talking about P-Firm and the bright prospects for this product in India. Everyone was very excited. It was after a very long time that a very successful global product is being launched in India. There is a special team being set up; she also announced some promotions and the hiring plans to drive P-Firm's growth.

11

Gurugram

Anirban Basu and his wife Srabani knew about their son's girlfriend. Their son, Nilanjan Basu was not at all secretive about his affair with Rina Khosla. Rina has been to their house twice – once during Nilanjan's birthday and then for Durga Puja.

Anirban spoke to Rina when she was at their place, and he came to know about some interesting stuff her brother was working on.

Rina told him, "He is trying to set up a company to create cloud-based software solutions for businesses." She shared more details based on whatever she heard from her brother.

The more he heard about her brother Puneet, the more impressed he was with his bold steps and efforts. Anirban always wanted to venture out into something of his own, but the comfort of his well-paying job always stood as a hindrance! But he felt it would be a good idea to get into some such venture as an early investor so that when the company grows one gets to reap the fruits.

Srabani was very impressed. She told Anirban, "It's amazing

that the youngsters are thinking of starting something on their own instead of working for someone."

Puneet was also looking for some early investors who can provide some guidance and the kind of freedom he required to explore the market and figure out some best solutions for his target segment.

Rina introduced Puneet to Anirban, and they met at Starbucks in Gurugram. Anirban was so impressed with the kind of clarity Puneet had about the things we wanted to do. He was very thorough in his domain and was connecting with lot of like-minded people through the VC circle.

Kwoley had given RSUs (Restricted Stock Units) to Anirban and the vesting of around 25% of his RSUs were due. The total value of his vested stocks would be Rs 1 crore. He felt that it would be a good idea to invest in Puneet's venture. His plan was to invest Rs 30 lakhs for 30% equity. They met again in Gurugram to discuss about the proposal.

San Francisco

The Twin Peaks – 2 uninhabited hills, more than 900 feet high, offers one of the finest views out over the city and bay. Rahul and Stephanie drove to the north peak parking area and soaked up the amazing vista.

To their surprise, there weren't many tourists. The weather was so good. Stephanie was in a good mood and wanted to have some fun. She knew Rahul is bit conservative when it comes to certain things – he doesn't do much of PDA, but things were very different when they are at home. He could really drive her crazy.

Rahul was also in a mood to chill, and he wanted to make it

a memorable day for his girlfriend. He looked at her. Her eyes allured and it was an invitation he couldn't resist.

The Twin Peaks are the only hills in San Francisco not to have been built over and remain in their original state. The Spaniards called them "Los pechos de la Chola" or the Breasts of the Indian Maiden. Even on warm days, strong, cool breezes blow in from the Pacific, especially in the late afternoon.

12

NDA Campus – Pune

Nilanjan Basu was so proud to be part of the Hunter Squadron, 2nd Battalion. His aim was to win the 'Best in Gliding' Trophy and prestigious Sqn Ldr Vasudev Memorial Book Prize. These prizes are normally awarded one night prior to the Passing Out Parade.

He told his friend Animesh, "The best thing I love about National Defence Academy is the AFTT (The Airforce Training Team)!"

This team focused on training the cadets in the basics of military aviation through ground training and flying training. Ground training is normally conducted with the help of modern training aids, aircraft models and cross-sectional models of aero engines.

Visits to Air Force training establishments, Air Force stations and civil aviation centers are also undertaken to give cadets first-hand experience of aviation activities. Flying training at the AFTT is fully backed by an Automatic Weather Station, Air Traffic Control Station, a paved runway, and dispersal for six aircrafts.

The AFTT was formed towards the end of 1956. The aim of the AFTT is to introduce the VI Term cadets to gliding and allied professional subjects, which in turn prepares them for their professional training in the Air Force flying establishments.

Over the last 60 years, gliding training has evolved into flying training. Five different classes of gliders were acquired by the Academy since 1957. They are Sedberg T-21B, Baby Eon, Eon Olympia, Rohini and Ardhra gliders. All these gliders except for the Baby Eon and Eon Olympia were utilized in the flying training of the cadets.

The Sedberg T-21B was the mainstay of the AFTT in glider flying with each cadet being permitted a total of 60 training launches, after which 2-3 mandatory Solo Check launches were flown with the Chief Flying Instructor. Cadets cleared for solo flying flew one solo trip on the glider and were then formally awarded their 'Wings', exactly half the size of the official India Air Force wings, which were worn above the left shirt pocket of their formal uniforms.

The cadet who went solo with the lowest number of launches was usually awarded the Best in Gliding Trophy on the guest dining-in night, one night prior to the Passing Out Parade.

Rina got a final year project with a jewellery designer in Mumbai, and she had to meet some of her team members in Pune. She was so excited that she will also get to meet Nilanjan.

She called Nilanjan to share the good news. He was so excited.

Rajesh and Ruchita were bit sad as she is leaving them for the first time.

Ruchita said, "Beta, try to come home whenever you get holidays instead of going out for trips with your friends." She was very possessive about Rina.

Rina was also very emotional while leaving Delhi. But she was happy that she will get to meet Nilanjan more often.

She had bought so many things from Delhi as she was meeting him after 2 years. Both really got busy with studies. She was so happy for Nilanjan that he got admission at the right place as he was so passionate about flying and always read stuff related to it. She remembered him pestering his father to get lot of simulator games when he was in school.

She was proud of Nilanjan, and she knew her parents and brother had lot of admiration for Nilanjan. Anirban, Nilanjan's father once told her, "I could only become a corporate guy working for firangi bosses. But I'm so proud of my son that he will be serving the nation. What more can a father ask for?"

Anirban's father had served in the Indian Army, so Nilanjan had some blood relation with Defence, and it was his dream to get into NDA.

Rina and Nilanjan met briefly during the weekend and those two hours they just forgot about their surroundings and drowned deep into their world. They just kept looking at each other's eyes holding hands. It was such a blissful moment for both.

13
Pune

Rina was so happy about her project. Her first day at Hira Designs was so productive.

She had a very good discussion with Neetu Sharma, the Chief Designer and her super senior from college.

Neetu said, "We have come up with a new product line to gravitate young and chic women of today with the philosophy of catering to the needs of independent women. The brand has tried to reflect its precision in the logo. The idea is to maintain a balance between tradition and modern chicness."

Rina liked the way she explained. She asked, "So when we did the trend study, what all aspects were considered?

Neetu said, "Good question! We considered every aspect like what term of stones is, materials, influences etc. It was not limited to jewellery, also other personal accessories with the overlap of technology. Art and design are closely related. However, functionality counts the most."

Rina agreed.

She said, "Modern connoisseurs view jewellery as a form of

self-expression and when they identify themselves to each unique narrative it elevates the value of the piece into an emotion."

Neetu smiled and said, "Absolutely! And price doesn't matter much at that point."

After a small break, they continued with the discussion about the design team structure. She was keen on reorganizing the team.

The design team is responsible for taking brief from CRM team for various client projects and work under the owner for taking approvals and creating new design concepts and collections. They also do the QC (Quality Check) and work with various teams to ensure the aesthetics and quality of the product.

Rina knew that she is joining a professional team and they are highly regarded in the industry. Neetu is one of the highflyers and working so closely with her is a great thing. She knew it will really add value to her resume.

At Hira Designs, the focus was on re-inventing and fusing crafts and handicrafts, allowing them to produce limited edition pieces, making each piece a bespoke creation.

The owner's criteria for the luxury product were very clear – It should be low in supply, limited edition or rare and high in cost, mostly because of the amount of time invested by skilled craftspeople. They were also very clear that it should suit modern lifestyles.

14
Pune

Neetu Sharma stayed in a 3 BHK house with her pet, Bruno. Her husband had gone to Dubai for a year to do a project for Citibank. She was kind enough to offer Rina to stay with her till she finds a place of her choice. The only condition was to have drinks with her on weekends. Rina happily agreed and accepted her invitation.

Rina's parents, Rajesh and Ruchita were also very relieved that she has a senior who will take care of her in Pune. They did not have any relatives or friends in Pune, but they knew their daughter is happy to work in Pune as Nilanjan is there.

One month later

Rina and Bruno became good friends. She started taking him for a walk in the morning. Neetu was away to attend a conference in Mumbai. Weekends were so relaxing, and she had planned to watch some Netflix series. She dialed Puneet as it was almost a week they haven't spoken.

After couple of rings, Trisha picked up the phone.

Trisha said, "Hello Rina, I was just thinking of calling you. You will live for another 100 years."

Rina responded, "That will be very tough!" She laughed and asked, "How are you? My brother is still sleeping?"

Trisha said, "Yes, He was working late last night. Had some calls with investors in the US."

Rina asked, "Oh ok. How are things shaping up?"

Trisha said, "He is madly after the NASDAQ dream! Let us see how it goes. We have hired couple of people in the US in last 3 months. They are all very confident that it can be done in next 18 months."

Rina was very happy to hear that. She responded, "Fingers crossed!"

The calling bell rang, and Rina said she will call later. Trisha said she will ask Puneet to call her.

Trisha and Puneet were living together in Gurugram. She was also helping him with lot of things in his company.

Trisha went to the washroom to freshen up. When she came back, she saw Puneet making tea.

She took some biscuits, and they had tea in the bedroom.

15
Chandigarh

Rajesh and his Zonal Training Head, Nikhil Baweja were travelling to their offices in Punjab and Haryana. They started the trip with a townhall in Ludhiana, which is one of their biggest offices in the region. Then they went to Chandigarh. Nikhil had organized a conference for all the trainers in his Zone at the Chandigarh office. Nikhil knew that Madhuri and Sarabjeet will take care of the logistics there and will put up a good show. Madhuri and Sarabjeet were the most enterprising people in his team, and they always looked forward to opportunities to really making a difference and driving some great initiatives for the team. Madhuri and the admin staff decorated the office grand enough to indicate that a big event is happening there. All the sales managers and agent advisors were also very happy that the Zonal training conference is happening in their office.

The awards for the best trainers were also announced and there was so much excitement in the air. Rajesh and Nikhil addressed all the employees and then they moved to the training room. Rajesh inaugurated the conference and set the expectation for the team –

To win at least 3 national awards. He felt that his regional training team is one of the best in the country on all the parameters. He encouraged them to make some strong waves at national level this time. He mentioned that if the team wins, he will take them on a 3 day offsite to Goa.

The team was super excited. Nikhil and team continued with the conference.

It was 5 pm. Rajesh had to travel to Ambala to meet the team there next day and he boarded the cab. On the way, he got a call from Puneet.

Rajesh said, "Hi Puneet, Sorry beta, I could not take your call in the morning. How are things going?"

Puneet responded, "They are extremely happy with our financials. Raised 5 crores yesterday. The highest in last couple of months."

"Wow! Amazing", said Rajesh. He continued, "Proud of you, beta! Did you call mom?"

Puneet said, "Yes, I called her an hour back." He added, "Trisha and I will have to travel to SFO next week to meet Charles and his team. Charles wants me to meet some of his partners as they might be interested as well."

Rajesh said, "Excellent! Neeta will be very happy! Hope you will get time to meet her and family. Rina is also settling down well in Pune. Spoke to her yesterday."

"Yes Dad, Trisha and I spoke to her. She is happy and you know the reason!" He smiled.

Rajesh laughed and said, "I'm so happy that my children have found their life partners themselves."

Puneet knew what his next question would be. His parents have been checking with him about marriage for some time now. But he felt he is not prepared for it.

He mentioned to his dad that someone has come to meet him, and he will call later.

Rajesh said, "Ok beta, let me know once you book the tickets. All the very best!"

Sonu, the driver of the cab was listening to their conversation.

Rajesh asked, "Aur kitna time lagega Sonu?"

Sonu is Rajesh's favourite driver. The office arranges Sonu's cab whenever Rajesh comes for a visit.

Sonu told Rajesh, "Sir ek ghanta lagega. Bahut traffic milta hai iss time par."

"Acha" responded Rajesh.

Rajesh asked him, "Aur kya chal raha hai?"

He responded, "Sir, bilkul theek hai. Papa bol rahe hain taxi wala kaam chodkar real estate mein dhyan lagane ko."

Rajesh smiled and said, "Kya baat hai! Sahi sector hai. Real estate sales mein acha commission milta hai."

Sonu responded, "Humara thoda zameen abhi sarkar ne leliya aur acha rate mila."

Rajesh asked, "Kitna mila?"

Sonu said, "Teen crore."

Rajesh didn't know how to react. After a pause, he laughed and said, "Bhaiyya, aapko ghar pe aaram karna chahiye. Kyu gaadi chala rahe ho." Rajesh had an expression of disbelief on his face.

Sonu laughed loudly. Then he asked Rajesh, "Maine suna hai insurance mein bhi investment ka option hai. Sahi hai Sir?"

Rajesh said, "Humare paas toh bahut tharah ke products hai. Insurance bhi lena chahiye abhi. Saath mein guaranteed return milne wala products bhi hai. Tumhare ghar par mein koi sales manager ko bhejtha hun."

Sonu said, "Theek hai Sir. Papa se discuss karke aapko batadenge."

Rajesh leaned back and he was lost in thoughts.

16
Pawna Lake and Napa Valley

Nilanjan and Rina felt so blissful as they spent some lovely time together. Adorned with the sheer bliss of nature, Pawna Lake camps showcase a lure which will promisingly entice any nature lover. Their campsite was situated on the lush green landscape alongside the banks of Pawna Lake, surrounded by misty valleys of the Western Ghat. The refreshing ambience made it a sought-after destination for couples.

With the sky dotted by the sparkling stars along with the soothing noise of the river water, the lake camp was an excellent escape from the chaos of the city life. Nilanjan and Rina really enjoyed the moments romancing under the starlit sky.

Nilanjan shared his excitement about joining Air Force Academy in Dundigal. The training will be for a year. Rina felt that their marriage can happen after 2 years so that she can also settle well in her job.

San Francisco

Puneet and Trisha were having a tough time in SFO. Puneet was so engrossed in his work as the investors were putting pressure to onboard more clients.

He told the technical team, "Let us enhance the platform with more features and bandwidth so that it looks classy for the prospective clients."

Puneet was working almost 18 hours a day. Trisha and her team were focusing on client onboarding. They literally did not have much time to think about anything else. It was just about work! Puneet and the investors really felt that the platform can be scaled a lot more before taking the company public.

During the weekend, they went to Napa Valley. Puneet's college batchmate, Tarun and his wife Amrita also joined them. Rahul suggested his favourite place, Castello di Amorosa to Puneet. Trisha was very fond of wines so he felt she would enjoy being there.

Four of them entered the grand castle and were seated in the courtyard. Wine began to flow into their glasses one bottle after another. They felt as if they were the only ones there. They loved the host, Chris who took them on a guided tour for wine and cheese tasting. He was incredibly funny, affable, and answered all their questions. They found the castle absolutely stunning and the history very fascinating. All of them had a lovely time at Castello di Amorosa.

Trisha called Rahul and thanked him for the suggestion. She loved that place.

Gurugram - One year later

Anirban Basu was so happy. He had tears in his eyes when he saw Ravinder Kumar cutting the cake celebrating his 10th year with Kwoley. The company gifted him a memento and a gold coin in appreciation of his work. Ravinder's journey is an inspirational one and more like a folklore which people hear when they join Kwoley.

Ravinder Kumar is an office support staff member who can impress any sales team member with his knowledge about Kwoley's titles. The only hurdle for him was that he doesn't know how to talk in English. Otherwise, Ravinder was widely considered as the walking dictionary of Kwoley's books as he could identify titles with names of authors, color codes on the covers and cover designs.

Ravinder came from a remote village in Rajasthan. His uncle brought him to Delhi at a very young age as he stopped his studies very early. His uncle was working for Kulwant Singh, a book seller in Darya Ganj.

Kulwant was looking for a domestic help as he wanted someone to help his wife to take care of their son. Ravinder was identified for that job, and he started staying with Kulwant's family. He was offered a monthly salary of Rs 150, and all other expenses were taken care of by Kulwant. Within a month, Kulwant and his wife were very impressed with Ravinder. Their kid also became very fond of him. He also learned cooking and started helping Kulwant's wife in the kitchen.

Kulwant started taking Ravinder's help at his bookstore. He regularly attended the New Delhi Book Fair at Pragati Maidan and displayed all the new titles there. Ravinder was the one responsible for setting up the stall and the book fair and doing all the backend work. He has been doing a good job of setting up things and giving publicity about the book titles in their stall.

Kulwant belongs to that category of people who cover up their shortcomings smartly with the sheer energy and passion to get things done. He started selling Kwoley's books and became their most preferred distributor in India. When the sales numbers started picking up, Kwoley leadership felt that it's time to launch their operations in India. They appointed Shrikant Lal, a veteran in the field of publishing as Managing Director. Kulwant was eyeing that position, but he could not make it. He was disappointed. The VP -Sales in New York was aware of his disappointment. He spoke to Shrikant and asked him to connect with Kulwant to get him as the Sales Director.

17
Auckland, New Zealand – Few months later

Mike Kohler and his girlfriend, Sarah Wilson were spending their second week in Auckland. Mike's father, James Kohler's best friend had decided to sell his beach house to Mike.

"It's a beautiful retreat with lot of surf spots." Sarah said.

"Being surrounded by a kwila deck including pergolas, it is accessible from numerous points. I feel it's a perfect place to entertain guests at different times of the day capturing sun and shade." Mike said.

Sarah said, "Displaying native timbers throughout highlighting the beauty with a modern rustic look, the whole house has a Wabi-Sabi feel to it."

She liked the place very much. The beach house situated 20 minutes away from the town, one could relish in the microclimate on deck listening to nature which surrounds the home.

"The deal is getting finalized on Monday. I'm so excited." Mike said.

Sarah conveyed the good news to her parents. It's been almost 5 years that Sarah and Mike have been dating.

This news was certainly a very exciting one for them and they were hopeful about the marriage soon.

Mike and Sarah planned to celebrate the deal closure with a big bang. They invited couple of friends.

They were couple of pegs down and were having a good time with their guests. He noticed his mobile ringing. It was Rahul. Mike didn't pick the call instead he messaged, "Busy, will call you later"

Mike met Rahul before leaving from Florida. He discussed about the possibility of an investment in his cousin's IT company.

Sarah and her friends were calling Mike for some tequila shots. They had couple of shots and then their friends started leaving. They all had a great time.

Mike and Sarah were so happy that they have become proud owners of a classy beach house in Auckland. Mike and Sarah walked into their extravagant bedroom. He caught hold of her shoulders, pulled her to him and planted an exuberant kiss on her lips.

They could hear the waves outside. The cocktail of love and alcohol created waves of ecstasy within.

Next day in the morning, Mike dialed Rahul.

Rahul said, "Good morning buddy, Congrats to you and Sarah! I would love to see your new beach house sometime soon."

Mike responded, "Anytime brother, it's a lovely place."

Rahul said, "Great! Any thoughts on what we discussed the other day?"

Mike answered, "Yes, I'm planning to give it a shot. Did some research and seems like they are doing well and there is amazing growth potential."

Rahul smiled, "Wow! That's great news! Hope I can tell Puneet about it. He will be very excited. You guys may want to get into a call as well."

Mike said, "Yes, Will talk to him when I'm back in Florida."

18

Puneet's flight to SFO was delayed. Every time his flight gets delayed, he gets a call with some good news. He was thinking that in the past 5 – 6 years, he has always received some or other good news whenever he is in the airport lounge. In his sister's words, Universe always gives a special sign and only few people can recognize the uniqueness of it.

He went to the bookstore at the New Delhi airport to check the new arrivals. He was about to pick up a book. His mobile rang. It was Rahul.

Puneet said, "Hi bro"

Rahul smiled and said, "I have a great news for you, bro! Mike is willing to invest!"

Puneet was pleasantly surprised. He said, "Wow! That's amazing! I had an intuition that some good news is going to come my way today. Usually, such things happen when my flight gets delayed." He smiled.

Rahul responded, "Mike has a deep pocket and can go upto 1 million. He will be back in Florida next week. You can connect with him. If things progress well, we can go ahead and acquire C-Soft"

Puneet was so happy to hear that. He knew that if Mike comes on board, the C-Soft deal can surely happen, and it will let the valuation soar in 6 months.

He told Rahul, "Sure. I will meet him when he is back in Florida. A client is looking for a lakefront estate in Orlando. I mentioned to him about Mike's project there. He seems to be interested. Maybe I will have some good news for Mike as well."

Rahul said, "Wow! That would be great! We need his dad's blessings as well. This should help."

Puneet and Rahul spoke a bit about the pitch, and they were confident about getting the much-needed investment from Mike.

Trisha was on her way to office. She called Puneet. He told her about the flight delay. She was asking him whether he got her favourite aloo bhujiya and bakarwadi from Haldirams. Puneet sent the pics of the items he bought from Haldirams. She sent him a big smiley and heart.

He told Trisha about Rahul's call. She was so happy to hear about the positive outcome. She had met Mike once during a party organized by Rahul and knew that he is a bigshot. A super rich guy!

She was missing Puneet as he has been away for almost a month.

His mom was hospitalized for 2 weeks so he wanted to be with her. Rina could not make it as she had to work on a design project in Paris for 2 months. The client was not ready to give her leave. Puneet knew that his dad won't be able to handle lot of stress as he was going through a tough phase professionally. So, he decided to be with mom and dad. Nilanjan also came to the hospital for 2 days to take care of his mother-in-law before he travelled to Pune.

Nilanjan and Rina had planned to travel to Paris and combine their honeymoon along with Rina's official visit, but Nilanjan had some urgent work-related commitments and could not travel with Rina.

Rajesh and Ruchita were so happy that their son and son-in-law could be with them in the hospital when they needed some support.

Nilanjan told them that he will be posted in Delhi for some time. This was a big relief for them.

19
Paris

Rina's client in Paris was a very demanding person. Rina had spent almost a month in Paris. Her schedule was so hectic that she could not squeeze out time for sightseeing.

Her boss, Caroline Garnier said, "French have a good taste for fashion, and this extends to jewelry."

Rina agreed, "From signet rings to ear cuffs to medallion pendant necklaces and tiny diamond drop earrings, they wear their jewelry pieces without effort."

Caroline responded, "Yes, France is home to some of the world's best ever jewelry designers."

Rina's boss had a very good understanding of the customer preferences as she was an experienced designer of Parisian jewelry. She had worked for some of the big names like Cartier, Van Cleef & Arpels and Maison De Grace.

She told Rina, "French women tend to prefer delicate, gold jewelry and simple vintage designs. A standard French girl jewelry collection might include two or three thin gold rings, a vintage pendant necklace and a set of simple gold hoop earrings."

Caroline always spoke passionately about her time in Maison De Grace. The Sultan of Brunei has been a loyal fan and patron of the brand, as is the Emir of Qatar.

Rina knew about their famed ring collections named Cleopatre and Socrate made of diamonds, precious stones, and palladium plated gold. These are the favourites of many royals across the world.

During the discussion she asked Rina, "Did you know that De Grace's family made mailboxes of gold and silver in the 1950s for the Vatican? Well that goes to show how exquisite this French jewelry brand is."

Puneet reached SFO. Trisha was in the airport to receive him. She was missing him so much and could not wait till he reaches home.

She gave him a tight hug as he got into the car.

She asked him, "How is mom now?"

Puneet said, "Much better. It might take some more time for her to get rid of the weakness."

He continued, "Dad has got an offer. He will have to join them next month."

She said, "Great news! I know he was really getting bored sitting at home."

He agreed. "Rina's wedding and other festivities kept him busy for 6 months but being a sales guy, he gets restless very soon. I have never seen him without a job for so long. He didn't take the 'Non-Compete' clause that seriously but then when he was about to join, they made a big issue out of it."

He was referring to the previous offer he had from DFC Bank. As DFC was planning to get into a strategic partnership with NYC Insurance, they introduced some strange clauses in the agreements. That messed up things for Rajesh but eventually things worked out for him.

20
Florida

Puneet, Trisha and Rahul travelled to Florida to meet Mike. In Orlando, Mike's family combined the best of private golf and lakefront living, suburban convenience, world class resort-style amenities and services. They passionately created a place where families and friends could build lasting memories in a new era of country club living.

From its longest tees, the luxury golf course measured more than 7,500 yards. Unique to Central Florida, the course featured open fairways and sweeping dunes amidst the area's natural hills and woodlands.

Mike and Sarah met them in their golf club.

After the initial conversation, Puneet and Rahul started discussing about the business expansion plans with Mike. Sarah took Trisha to the pool side, and they started having cocktails.

"As you have gone through the financials, let me share details about the planned acquisition which will take the company to the next league." Puneet said. He explained the C-Soft deal to Mike.

Mike was excited about the plans. Meeting Puneet and Rahul

helped him clearly understand the pros of the SAAS business model.

"The recurring revenues through subscription model and the scalability is very appealing" Mike said.

Puneet smiled and said, "It also allows for lot of different low-cost marketing strategies including side project marketing and affiliate marketing."

Mike felt there is an opportunity to build a team exclusively for the real estate business line as his father's company had projects globally.

He was happy to see the way SAAS model creates stickiness and loyalty, keeping the same customers for years. Mike also felt that Puneet and Rahul have built up a large enough user base to break even and move towards profitability. The only worry was about the new players contributing to increased competition all the time. But he felt that could be managed by building a loyal user base.

Their meeting went on for three hours. Mike and Sarah invited them for lunch at their grand Tuscan-inspired Clubhouse. Their Chef is so famous for putting a modern spin on the classics, drawing inspiration from local farms and Florida's coasts. Everyone loved the food, and they kept chatting for next few hours.

Puneet liked Mike's suggestion for building a different segment focused on real estate. Tarun Malik, his collegemate was doing something similar at a small scale in Delhi and he felt there would be some opportunities to build synergy there and slowly consider acquiring his company.

Mike told them that he will stick to the figure he quoted to Rahul initially.

"Let us go aggressive and close the C-Soft deal which means

getting 1000+ customers on board." Puneet said. He saw it as a huge opportunity to enhance the user experience and venture into new domains.

"The good thing with C-Soft is they have a growing user base and enhancing their product would mean some extra dollars as revenue in terms of premium." Rahul said.

He knew that their customers won't mind paying a premium as they are glued to the product for many years now.

21
Mumbai

Rajesh's induction program went well. He met Manish Seth, Chief Distribution Officer at Moon Life Insurance. Manish is a good friend of Rajesh's ex-boss, Amardeep Singh Lamba.

"Amardeep has told me great things about you." Manish said.

He continued, "I feel that we have not succeeded in making inroads in the Agency distribution model in Punjab, Haryana, and Himachal Pradesh. That is where I need your help."

Manish knows NYC Life did some amazing numbers through the agency model in these geographics. His objective behind hiring Rajesh was to design a strategy to penetrate these markets and establish a strong agency model. Manish knew that Rajesh is one of the most respected leaders in the insurance domain and he enjoys a loyal following of insurance sales folks in these states.

Puneet called Rajesh in the evening to check how his first day went. From Rajesh's tone, he could sense that his father has liked the new workplace.

He shared the news about Mike's investment in the company. Rajesh was excited.

He was delighted to hear that Puneet might plan another visit to Delhi very soon as he had to meet Tarun Malik and discuss the possibilities of building a superior platform to cater to Mike's real estate customers.

Mike was keen on building a new platform and leverage the connections through his personal network and the startup ecosystem in SFO through the help of Puneet and Rahul. Mike had developed a certain level of confidence on both.

Nilanjan's father, Anirban Basu, being a long-term investor in Puneet's company always spoke so proudly about his investment and the company's growth. He was also aware of the latest plan to raise funds from Mike.

His colleague Kulwant, the Sales Director in Kwoley had received a lot of money by way of inheritance by selling the family property in Patiala. Anirban was aware that he was considering investing in real estate in Delhi. But he wanted to guide him and get him to invest in Puneet's company as he saw a bright future. Anirban himself was super impressed with the way things were progressing.

Kulwant said, "I want to donate some portion of the proceeds from my inheritance to Ravinder's new project to support some self-help groups in Rajasthan." Ravinder and some of his friends collaborated with an NGO to generate funds to ensure economic empowerment of landless and marginalized families through some skilling initiatives.

He continued, "The skilling initiatives are focused on two projects - honey production and providing assembling support for some solar energy companies."

Kulwant knew that Ravinder will leave Kwoley someday to entirely focus on this noble cause to support so many marginalized people. He wanted to support Ravinder as he has done a lot for Kulwant's family.

Ravinder has gone through lot of hardships in life, and he felt so grateful for the opportunities to connect with so many influential and rich people like Kulwant and Anirban.

It was a very big thing for an uneducated guy from a remote village in Rajasthan to land in a multinational corporation and get to a place where everyone respects him for the value he adds in his own way. Even the CEO of Kwoley India complimented Ravinder for his product knowledge.

Ravinder went to his village once in a year for 2 weeks and it was mostly during Diwali. Most of the people in his village lived in circular huts with thatched roofs and walls covered with plaster of clay, hay, and cow dung. Affluent zamindars living in larger villages owned bigger houses.

From transport to ploughing, the villagers depended on camel. Even the postman brought the mails on the back of a camel. Even though there was electricity, the supply was always interrupted. The kerosene lamps still illuminated in the night. The children ran around freely and studied in an open-air school.

22

Pune – 10 months later

"A test pilot's mind is stuffed with mathematics and engineering concepts, but his life is filled with adrenaline and adventure," said Sunil Tandon, Nilanjan's favourite senior.

Nilanjan said, "It's so true! One of the greatest charms of test-flying is that you can fly any aircraft! Test pilots fly various aircrafts over their careers, pushing the envelope to ensure that the machine is put through its paces and ready for operational use."

Nilanjan was fully aware of the pressure and complexity in his role but chose to be there for the sheer passion of flying and for being part of the group that only a few make it to.

"The test pilots are experienced aviators – a glorious blend of pilot, aeronautical engineer and scientist," continued Sunil.

They are trained to fly and evaluate experimental, newly produced or modified aircraft using certain maneuvers called flight test techniques.

They are trained to fly any aircraft and need to adapt to varied cockpit environments — from fighter jets to passenger planes, transport aircraft to microlights. Teamwork is essential, working closely with flight-test engineers to create an end product that can safely be inducted into operational use.

Production test pilots test new machines that come off the assembly line. An experimental test pilot has these qualifications, but also the more nuanced skills to test prototypes and is involved in the process right from the time the first line is drawn, their inputs are critical to the designing of the machine. With excellent communication skills, they need to be able to think from the perspective of not just a pilot, but also an engineer.

San Francisco

Mike and Sarah started taking great interest in the affairs of the company. Puneet also welcomed Mike's involvement in the day-to-day functioning of the company. He was glad to see the interest Mike is taking in the business.

Puneet said, "Before diving into the details of pricing, branding, or building a team, it's important to make sure you have a clear problem to address and solution that alleviates it. After all, if you are not solving a problem, you don't have a business."

Mike's view was also very similar. He also believed that if you can fix a problem for someone and do it better, quicker, and cheaper than your competitor, you are off to a good start.

Beyond knowing your customers well, it's also important to know your competitors. The presence of your competitors in your market is a good thing. It means a problem has in fact been identified. The trick then is figuring out what part of your competitor's solution is inadequate. What do customers want that they don't currently get?

Puneet explained to Mike, "The subscription-based pricing model is the popular model for SAAS companies because of the increased potential lifetime value – like $240 for the single sale opportunity you have with each customer or user, you might charge $20 per month per user for as long as your customer uses your service."

Mike responded, "Yes, the longer they stick around, the higher their lifetime value."

After going through the sales forecast and budget related documents, Mike understood that Puneet and his finance guy have done a very good job with it.

Without a real sales forecast and budget, you have no idea how much money you are going to need to get your business off the ground. After all, with the subscription business, you are only going to get a small payment every month from each customer, and you don't know how long the customers are going to subscribe.

23
Sonepat, Haryana

Rajesh received a call from his Regional HR Head in Delhi. He mentioned about an incident in Sonepat where the branch head and the HRBP were threatened by an employee. The labour officer also got involved as the employee threatened both when they were in the labour office. Rajesh immediately called his friend Balwinder, a SHO in Karnal police station. He gave a brief about the incident. Balwinder called the SHO in Sonepat and informed about this case. By that time, the branch head and the HR person had reached the police station and they were filling the FIR.

This employee was not attending the office for a while. He was putting in some money from his salary monthly to buy insurance policies and was getting those policies cancelled in the free look period. He smartly managed to get the policy logins from his office and get the cancellations done from some office in Delhi. This way he managed to get incentives for the policy logins. It was found out by the agency standards team, and they alerted the branch head. As he did not get any satisfactory explanation from the employee, they decided to take the required disciplinary action. That is when the employee decided to go to the labour office.

When the discussions were going on with the labour officer, he felt that his case doesn't have any merit and out of anger he threatened the branch head and the HR person.

Finally, at the police station he decided to submit the resignation as there was no way he could have continued in the company.

Rajesh received an update that the person has resigned. He was relieved.

He received a call from Vinay Gulati, his ex-colleague from NYC Life Insurance.

After greeting him, Vinay said, "Sir, I want to share a great news with you. My daughter has received an offer from SmartSaaS in the US. I know it's your son's company. She told me great things about the company. So proud of him."

Rajesh responded, "Wow! Great news, Vinay! It's a small world!"

Vinay said, "Absolutely, very small world!"

Rajesh said, "I still remember that schoolgirl who asked lots of questions to you. Kids grow up so fast."

Vinay was so happy to hear it from Rajesh.

They spoke for half an hour. Vinay shared some interesting updates from NYC Life and Rajesh also had lot of exciting things to share about his new company.

Vinay's daughter, Ekta was working in a Bangalore based software company. She also did some modelling assignments while working in Bangalore. She did well as a model as quite a few ad agencies preferred her. But she only spent weekends for the modelling assignments as her aim was to start a software company in few years.

Her bosses were super impressed with her work and her knowledge about the domain. She was sent to SFO to work for a client. She ended up spending 6 months there. She saw a job posting by SmartSaaS and applied for it.

She had couple of interviews and finally received an offer. She was happy with the package offered. She informed her parents about it and that is when Vinay remembered that SmartSaaS in his ex-boss's son's company.

24

New York and San Francisco

Puneet moved to New York for a year to take care of some key projects for some prestigious clients there.

Sarah went to Auckland for some work.

Ekta started reporting to Mike as she was tasked to launch some new features on the platforms for the real estate clients. Mike was a tough boss but gave lot of insights to the team about the nuances related to the sector. Ekta had a team of 3 people supporting her on the technical side.

Mike and Ekta both travelled a lot and met lot of clients. They started developing a fondness for each other.

One day they were discussing about some specifications shared by a client at Mike's office in Orlando. There was a gentle pause between the conversation. Her eyes flew open, and he saw raw desire in the mystical depths. He was too close to miss it, too attentive to misread the stark longing for anything but the true passion it was.

Not willing to lose the moment, he claimed her mouth, drawing the desire back to the surface. She melted against him, sinking into the kiss.

He asked her, "Why don't we go upstairs where we can be more comfortable and have some good fun?"

She smiled. They went upstairs. The view from there was awesome.

Mike started complimenting Ekta, "You are a very intelligent and creative techie. I just love your passion for technology."

"I'm convinced that you will be able to help me develop a platform that enables real estate owners and managers to change how people experience and use rental space," Mike had said.

She responded, "Sure Mike. We will develop a platform which can give a good idea to the clients about asset performance, leveraging the data insights and ways to monetize space to create incremental yields."

From a sales and marketing perspective, he had good exposure into managing marketing through multiple channels where owners can capture leads effectively at a lesser cost.

Ekta came up with ideas about more features under the gamut of property management like automating the leasing and renting, also the management and accounting aspects. She also shared some brilliant tech ideas about optimizing the rents to achieve the highest yield.

The frequency of calls between Mike and Sarah came down significantly. Whenever Sarah called, half of the time he did not pick up the calls. If he picked the call, it was to tell her that he is busy in a meeting.

He ensured Ekta stayed with him. His father could sense that something is brewing. His father also interacted with Ekta a lot and felt that she is real beauty with brains.

Mike's father was amazed to see the progress Ekta and Mike made in developing a great platform which could really take their business to a different league. Puneet had some other pet projects, so he was focusing on the acquisitions. He was happy with the partnership with Mike as he felt there is a credible product line which is coming up with Ekta at the helm of real estate tech in their company.

25

San Francisco - One year later

Ekta was promoted as VP – Product Development and she was gaining popularity as a tech leader internally and externally. She won one of the most prestigious awards in the tech space. Her love affair with Mike went solid. Mike's family wanted him to settle down with Ekta.

Sarah started getting very cold vibes from Mike and she was smart enough to understand that he has found someone. Mike had transferred the beach property he bought in Auckland to Sarah some time back. She developed a very good bond with Trisha after their meeting in Florida. They spoke to each other very often. Sarah knew that Trisha would know more about the latest developments in Mike's life.

Sarah once mentioned to Trisha, "Ask Puneet to be careful. Mike may just snatch away his company."

Trisha replied, "Puneet is a hardcore techie and is so passionate about this business and people. And Mike partners with him very well. I'm sure that they know staying together is beneficial to both."

Sarah continued, "Mike's family has done this kind of stuff to lot of people in the real estate business. That is how they grew their business. Just thought of cautioning you."

Trisha tried to shift the topic. She knew that Sarah is very upset with Mike as he has started ignoring her. She felt bad for her but did not take her comments very seriously.

Puneet was so engrossed in the process of onboarding 2 big clients from the banking sector. He kept shuttling between New York and San Francisco. He formed a core team of 2 VPs, 5 data scientists and 30+ techies. Ekta reached out to Puneet whenever she needed support on the tech side. She worked closely with Mike's core team.

During the weekend, Puneet and Trisha went for a tour combining three of the Bay Area's top attractions – Alcatraz Island, Muir Woods and Sausalito. They enjoyed the comfortable transportation in a luxury tour van, which included a trip across the Golden Gate Bridge, allowing them to focus on the scenery instead of the driving and directions. The Alcatraz admission included the ferry ride and the audio tour. They had lot of free time to explore Muir Woods and Sausalito. It was a much-needed break.

Trisha was tempted to share with Puneet what Sarah told her. But she did not want to distract Puneet as he was so focused on several important projects with Mike. She did not want to plant any seed of suspicion in his mind.

26
Egypt and New York

Nilanjan received his second promotion after joining Airforce. Rina was elated. He was posted in Chief of Air Staff's office. After the first week in the office, he joined the core team which planned Chief of Air Staff's (CAS) visit to Egypt to attend the Air Power Symposium and Egyptian Defense Exposition.

The CAS was invited by the Egyptian Air Force Commander to deliver a keynote address on strategic air intelligence in confronting new and non-organized threats.

Rina knew that Nilanjan was a big fan of the new CAS. He mentioned great things about him when the CAS flew solo in a Mig-21 fighter jet a year back.

Nilanjan and Rina's son, Abhinav was with his grandparents as Rina had to travel for a show organized by a French luxury brand.

In Egypt, Nilanjan had an excellent opportunity to connect with some of the big wigs in the establishment. He became the blue-eyed boy of the seniors in a very short time. Everyone loved him for his intelligence and meticulous planning. His track record was so great that he was given responsibilities which would have normally gone to people with lot of experience.

Puneet's projects in New York went in full swing. He and his team did an amazing job there and they were so optimistic about winning another big client from the banking sector. He knew that he is just one step away from listing the company in NASDAQ. Everything was going as per the plan.

NASDAQ – 2 years later

Puneet was live on ET Now and he was mentioning to the journalist that it feels like day zero all over again. He was telling the journalist about the billion-dollar market opportunity and his plans to scale the business.

Puneet and Mike rang the opening bell, which was streamed on the screen in Times Square, New York.

A prominent investor in the SaaS space was quoted saying, "It's going to stiffen the spine and provide immense belief that we can build very large $50 billion-plus companies from India by building products in India for the world."

Puneet's tweet followed. He wrote, "Today is a dream come true for me – from humble beginnings in Delhi to ringing the bell at Nasdaq. Big thanks to our employees, customers, partners, and investors for believing in this dream."

The listing will also benefit more than half of the 5000 employees of his company who have employee stock options. To the question on stock options, Puneet responded that close to 3000 of our employees in India will be crorepatis and 2500 of them are under the age of 30. He smiled.

He had told Trisha few years back that he is not starting

SmartSaaS for him to buy a Merc, he is starting it so that all his employees can buy Mercs. He felt that he is delivering on that promise.

Puneet launched the company 10 years back after reading an article on how customer support and sales communication platform Metdesk's clients were unhappy after it raised its prices by 300%. He teamed up with his friend for many years, Karthik, to offer customers a competing and effective product at a lower price. Then Rahul joined him in SFO, and Mike became an investor. They launched new platforms.

Puneet's company, SmartSaaS raised its first $1 million in funding from XL ventures and 5 years later when it raised $250 million from XL Ventures and GM Partners, it became the country's first SaaS firm to be valued at over $2 billion.

27
Sulur Air Force Station – One year later

The Russian built Mi-17 medium lift helicopter was ready for its maiden flight with the VVIP after its most recent servicing. Wing Commander Deepak Singh, the commanding officer of 120 Helicopter Unit, was the pilot in command, with co-pilot Squadron Leader Amit Bakshi and two junior warrant officers comprising the rest of the crew.

Nilanjan was among the CAS staff travelling to Defence Services Staff College (DSSC) where the CAS was to address the college's faculty and student officers. The passengers boarded the flight around 11:45 am.

At 11:48 am, the helicopter took off with 8 passengers including the Chief of Air Staff and 4 crew members from Sulur Air Force Station headed roughly 80 km to the DSSC in Wellington, Tamil Nadu. The helicopter was scheduled to arrive at Wellington by 12:15 pm. Around 12:08 pm, the pilots radioed air traffic control to confirm their imminent landing at the Wellington helipad. Immediately after that, they lost contact with the Sulur Air Force base.

Murugan, an employee of a private tea estate near Bandishola was at his home. He did not go for work that day as he had high fever. He suddenly heard a loud noise and ran outside his home to see what was happening.

There were plumes of smoke, and he could see lot of people running. A helicopter had hit the tree and was on fire. In few minutes, the fire was higher than Murugan's house. The villagers – most of them tea estate employees, threw water over the fire in attempt to put it out.

IAF rushed its team with ambulances to the crash site as soon as they received information about the crash. IAF officially confirmed Chief of Air Staff's presence on the helicopter in a tweet at 2 pm. The Fire and Rescue Services personnel managed to reach the crash site after some difficulty, as the site was 500 meters from the major road. They saw the crash victims and they were all burnt beyond recognition.

The Cabinet Committee on Security (CCS) headed by the Prime Minister planned for an urgent meeting to review the situation. The Parliament was in session and the Defence Minister asked his team to put together a statement as he had to make the formal address and give an update to all the MPs about the crash.

Nilanjan was the initial survivor of the crash and was taken to the military hospital in Wellington for the surgery. Having sustained burns over 45% of his body, he was transferred to the Command Hospital in Bengaluru for further treatment on life support.

Romil and Nidhi helped Rajesh and family a lot during this extremely difficult phase. As Romil was politically very connected, he could mobilize a lot of things really fast.

Romil and his wife Nidhi always saw Rajesh as their mentor and well-wisher. Rajesh supported Romil and Nidhi during his tenure as Zonal Sales Director at NYC Life Insurance Company several times and they won several accolades under his leadership. Romil and Nidhi were the most pampered agent advisors in the EC Club and they qualified for many foreign trips. Rajesh helped a lot in convincing their parents about the marriage as there were some initial hiccups.

There had been a deluge of wishes and messages for Nilanjan, who was the only one to be pulled out alive after the helicopter crash. Entire country was praying for Nilanjan. Anirban described his son as a fighter.

Everyone had a tough time consoling Nilanjan's mother Srabani, Rina and Abhinav. It was too much for Rina and she didn't know what to do. She never felt so helpless as Nilanjan continued to be critical, on life support for more than ten days.

The Defence minister spoke to Anirban about the health condition of Nilanjan and he ensured the best medical support to bring him back to life.

28

San Francisco – One year later

Ekta and Mike were celebrating their first wedding anniversary. After the celebrations with family and colleagues, they headed to their most favorite beach property. While enjoying the wine closer to the beach, Ekta was looking at Mike intently. He was enticing. She walked up to him and kissed him, flush on his lips. He kissed her back. Softly, he sank her on to the sand. The sea water slithered in under her, tickling her as it flowed back into the sea, drawing out sand from underneath. She wrapped her hands around him and drew him towards her.

They made love passionately. The sea waves kept lapping ardently against the shore.

Mike and Puneet were not getting along well.

"I feel Puneet is in his own world and has lost the larger focus of taking the organization to the next level. The real estate domain was contributing almost 70% of the revenue." Mike told Ekta.

He continued, "Puneet is not finding time to cater to the extraordinary needs while running a public company."

Puneet was so disturbed by the sudden demise of Nilanjan

and had to focus on supporting his sister, Rina and her son. Rina went into depression and had to be on medication for few months. Puneet had to travel a lot as he had to be with his parents and help Rina come out of the shock.

Mike told Ekta, "It's better to take the company private so that I can have a better control on things."

He knew that on the technology side he is well placed with the support from Ekta. She was so passionate about the business and always delighted customers with add on features on their platforms which helped in deriving immense value.

They had few meetings with their industry mentors and some high placed shareholders. They all could feel that Mike badly wanted to get full control over the company. And lot of them knew about Mike's family and their background.

Puneet and Trisha could not believe that Sarah's prophecy was coming true. Their own company which they built over a long period of time, brick by brick was being snatched away.

Mike had the prowess to really arm twist and get things in his favour and he did not leave any stone unturned. He knew that taking the current technology platform to the next level will help him enhance the prospects of his family business. They also had lot of real estate data across the country which positioned them at the pinnacle of their domain.

He and his powerful buddies on the board went directly to the shareholders, paid a premium for the shares, added in contingent value rights and made a quick move to acquire the company. Puneet was kept in the dark and he was not fully aware of the details.

Mike was so thankful to Ekta for her help to strengthen their offerings, which really brought them to a very enviable position.

Ekta had a meteoric rise in the company, and she was given greater responsibilities. Her income rose in an exceptional way.

She bought an amazing villa for her parents in Gurugram. The villa cost her INR 7.5 crores. She also bought a luxury car for them. Vinay Gulati and his wife were on top of the world.

29
Jaipur

Hawa Mahal, the five storied pyramidal edifice constructed out of red and pink sandstone is among the most popular tourist places to visit in Jaipur. Built by Maharaja Sawai Pratap Singh in 1799, it features 953 small windows and looks like a honeycombed hive. The interior chambers of this building enjoy a cooling effect due to the breeze blowing through its incredible lattice of windows.

But it was so warm outside. Ravinder's office is very near to Hawa Mahal.

Ravinder's team were busy setting up couple of projects to support water supply and sanitation in surrounding villages of Jaipur. They had started getting aids from the government agencies and some private companies as part of their CSR initiatives. Their projects included setting up electric pump sets to supply water for irrigation, conducting swachta program in villages, construction of drainage system for the adopted villages and construction of public toilets.

Ravinder felt that there is a lot to be done as he was getting lot of queries from the private players as everyone wanted to enroll his NGO as the CSR partner.

One day, he called Anirban as he needed his advice to scale up. Anirban had always taken very deep interest in the projects Ravinder was involved in. He also felt that there is a lot to be done as there was great support from the government and private players. Apart from giving his suggestions to identify some meaty projects, Anirban also mentioned about a recent conversation he had with Puneet.

He said, "One of Puneet's clients, a leading US based NGO is interested in taking up some projects in India, specifically in remote villages. I suggested him to connect with you."

Ravinder was excited. He knew that Puneet also has great interest in these initiatives as he had made some donations from his company when he started the NGO.

San Francisco

Puneet and Trisha were discussing about the various options in front of them. They knew the exit package will be good.

But they were very upset with the way things were going.

He told Trisha, "Its so depressing to see everything going away so soon. All my efforts to save it is going in vain."

Trisha said, "I agree with what you said the other day. We did a mistake by getting Mike into the company. It was the easy route to raise money that time but it certainly backfired."

"He had his agenda for sure. I knew it from the beginning. I tried to give him space and focus on things which matters for long term growth in all the domains we are in. I didn't want to get into unnecessary ego hassles." Puneet responded.

Puneet knew that even if things did not go in the right direction and if he had to move out of his company, SFO is the place to stay as it provided the right ecosystem. But he also had doubts whether to continue with SAAS setups or take up something new.

The conversation he had with the US based NGO was very interesting and he was thinking of pursuing it. They wanted someone on the ground, and he knew Ravinder can be a good partner to help him set up base in India and scale up further if he opted for that route. It looked more promising to him.

30
Florida

Things were not happening the way Puneet thought. He was becoming so aloof in his own company. Mike and his powerful friends arm twisted him in a way he did not have any other option – The only option was to quit. The exit package was good, so he did not want to fight back and spoil things further as everyone was on a serious ego ride.

Puneet also felt that it's time to explore something else.

He told Trisha, "It's not worth it. It is getting murkier day by day. I don't have the firepower to fight Mike and his family. They are well connected."

Trisha agreed. She told him, "Ekta is also unable to understand what went wrong. Seems like Mike doesn't want to discuss anything with her about it."

She continued, "I think he just wants to focus on the real estate domain. But he is stupid. Things can go seriously wrong if the market tumbles. Why he wants to put all the eggs in one basket?"

Puneet said, "No use talking to him. He will never understand."

He paused. Then said, "We did a big mistake. Getting him on board was a big mistake. But no point talking about it. I need to be careful next time."

Trisha knew that he is very upset as Mike literally snatched the company away. It's a big scar but she knew something much better is coming their way.

New Delhi

Rina's work kept her busy and that was the only way to get some relief from the pain of Nilanjan's absence. Her son, Abhinav was with his grandparents, Rajesh and Ruchita. He spent the weekends with Nilanjan's parents.

Abhinav's cricketing lessons were going well, and he was really enjoying it. Rajesh wanted to make Puneet a cricketer, but he became a techie.

Now Rajesh wanted to try his luck with his grandson. Things were working out well and the coaches in the cricket academy always kept very high benchmarks for Abhinav.

Cricket always helped him to forget the pain of losing his father at a very early age. His mother immersed herself in work and kept travelling always so he did not get much time from his mom. His grandparents, Rajesh and Ruchita were like strong pillars of strength. They always made sure that all his needs are taken care of. Nilanjan's parents, Anirban and Srabani also pampered Abhinav and did not want him to feel the absence of his father.

Abhinav had a fantastic relationship with Puneet and Trisha. They took him once to San Francisco. He had a very good time there.

From the iconic sights like the Golden Gate Bridge, to its rich and diverse culture, Abhinav understood that there are lots of places and people that made San Francisco unique. He fell in love with the city and its special vibes.

Puneet and Trisha took him to lots of restaurants so that he gets to taste delicacies from different parts of the world. Puneet told him that people in SFO always had a discerning taste, meaning culinary creators are always upping the game. The city is full of Michelin Star winning restaurants. San Francisco restaurants and chefs have been a driving force in global culinary innovation for decades.

Abhinav tasted everything from dim sum to burritos to sushi. He knew that no matter which type of cuisine one was craving for, one can find a San Francisco restaurant that satiates every unique need!.

31

Paris

Rina was eagerly waiting for her holiday after the Paris houte couture – a season linked with jewelry, from start to finish.

There were nearly 30 official couture shows on the Federation schedule during the week, but almost as many jewelry launches, displays, dinners and exhibitions in Paris.

Mega marques like Boucheron and Louis Vuitton had presentations, and the city had a plethora of smaller jewelry displays. In effect, the season began and ended with major jewelry statements by Chanel and Fendi, respectively.

Over the weekend, Chanel invited private clients for tours of the show, echoing Mademoiselle Chanel's dream of "covering women in a constellation of stars."

She overheard a famous editor, "Featuring well more than 100 million euros of jewelry, with a jazz band serenading guests and VIPs feting at the dinner. Though quite why the wealthiest luxury fashion brand on the planet cannot manage to serve turbot warm to guests will remain something of a mystery."

Everyone laughed.

New Delhi and Goa

Rajesh and Ruchita were so excited that the family is getting together after so many years to celebrate Diwali. After Nilanjan's demise, they did not take much interest in celebrating the festival. But this time it was special. Puneet, Rina and Trisha planned their travel in such a way that they could be with family for the festival. Ruchita's sister, Neeta, her husband Adi and son Rahul were also in Delhi. Abhinav was so delighted to have the company of all of them.

Rajesh planned things well for the five-day long festival beginning with Dhanteras extending up to Bhai Dooj. The cleaning was in full swing few days before Dhanteras. The family performed special pujas dedicated to Goddess Lakshmi. They decorated the house with candles, lamps, flowers and rangolis.

Neighbours and relatives came over as they knew it was a special Diwali for Rajesh and family. They exchanged gifts and sweets. Abhinav and his uncle were busy bursting crackers.

Puneet said, "A much-needed break!"

He had gone through a lot during the last few months, and it has been grueling both on professional and personal side.

Rina agreed. "Yes, a much-needed break for all of us. This time I'm detaching myself completely from work."

She hugged her son Abhinav and said, "Want to spend some quality time with him."

Abhinav smiled.

She knew he was missing her, but she was confident that he was well taken care of by both his grandparents.

After Diwali, they all went to Goa for a week. They had a great time – from beach walk early in the morning, hiring boats and going for dolphin spotting, to going on a road trip exploring the countryside – to camping in the forest, dusting off family lore and having few drinks to loosen tongues that spill out secrets!

When it came to food, Abhinav encouraged them to try everything and be a little adventurous. They explored homegrown restaurants that dot the roads, stylish cafes that offer world cuisine and fusion dishes, and of course, the shacks on the beaches that cooked excellent seafood meal with the day's fresh catch.

32

New Delhi – 6 months later

Puneet and his wife moved their base from SFO to Delhi. As he got a hefty exit package from Mike, he made some real estate investments. He also gifted a car to his parents.

He was clear about the cause his NGO will work upon. He had some likeminded people like Ravinder and Shreya Bansal (Puneet's batchmate from college) with him who did not wish monetary gains out of this initiative. They started putting together a team to help them prepare a memorandum that describes everything from the mission of the NGO and other details. The source of funding for the NGO was also identified. 2 SFO based NGOs were ready to support Puneet in his new venture.

Based on the research, some initiatives to conserve water bodies was his immediate focus area.

Natural water bodies such as lakes and ponds are source of drinking water. They help to control floods, support biodiversity and regenerate groundwater. With Indians already facing a severe water crunch, predicted by the scientists to worsen by 2030, he felt it is imperative to take action.

He presented some of his findings based on research to Shreya, Ravinder and the core team. These were alarming statistics.

He said, "Over 80% of crude sewage is discharged into water bodies. The number of lakes in India is continuously diminishing. Bangalore had nearly 260 lakes in the 1960s, now there are hardly 80."

He continued, "2001 data showed more than 135 lakes in Ahmedabad. Within 10 years, the numbers were less than 75. Hyderabad has lost more than 3200 hectares of wetlands in the past 15 years."

Shreya responded, "And the saddest part is that no one is concerned. We are just waiting for a disaster to happen to set things right."

"Despite some regulations and programmes in place, the condition of lakes in India is not improving much. National Wetlands Conservation Programme was established in 1985-86 to provide financial assistance for the protection of more than 100 wetlands in the country. However, nothing much happened as without the support of the state and Centre, even the environmentalists can't do much!" She read out from a document.

Puneet was very bullish. He knew that if they can pull off some consistent initiatives, its going to grab a lot of attention and more people will join the movement.

He said, "Let us start identifying the dying lakes in 3-4 states and bring them back to life. It will also help people fight the shortage of water."

They formed a 'Revive Lakes' team consisting of 50 volunteers. They tirelessly worked towards cleaning the lakes and spreading awareness among people in the vicinity. Within next 3 months, their flagship project - Vipura Lake Project in Bengaluru involved more than 250 volunteers, which helped the lake get rid of more than 5,000 kgs of garbage. Following the clean-up, the team also conducted door-to-door campaigning to create awareness about conserving the water body and keeping its surroundings clean. They also conducted tree plantation drives in and around Bengaluru.

The volunteers really enjoyed working with Puneet, Shreya and Ravinder. They were very different from many other NGO people. They were completely involved in the initiatives and could garner a lot of attention for this work through social media. They could also connect well with the local politicians to get their support for the project.

33
Sehwag Cricket Academy

The foundation of Sehwag Cricket Academy was laid by the 'Sultan of Najafgarh' himself with the sole aim of providing quality cricket training, world-class cricketing infrastructure, and the opportunity to learn from experts in the field of cricket through a fun and innovative environment. The flagship cricket academy was founded on the 23-acre eco-friendly campus at Jhajjar, on the outskirts of Gurugram in 2011, with an emphasis to provide students with best-in-class cricket facilities and training.

Rajesh was talking to Sanjay Mishra, his ex-colleague and cricket enthusiast, while driving to the Cricket Academy to pick Abhinav. He had lot of good words for Sehwag's Academy.

Rajesh told him, "For the overall development of the young cricketers, it is very important to focus on strength improvement through other games like swimming, tennis, and football. This can be done well by organizing mini tournaments and through sessions with specialists based on the ability, age group and expertise level of the players."

Sanjay said, "Yes, the Cricket Academy does a great job through some holistic development programs for young cricketers. They manage to get lot of Ranji-level players to coach them. I would love to see Abhinav playing for India."

Rajesh smiled. He was so happy to hear it from Sanjay. He said, "Yes, that is my dream. Let us see how things progress."

When Rajesh reached the Academy, Abhinav was batting the balls thrown by the bowling machines and the video analysis was going on. These sessions happen from time to time to help the boys understand the finer points of their game.

Abhinav saw a lot of value in the video analysis sessions. Sometimes recommendations given can be as simple as a change in the posture or a shift in focus of attention during a moment while at other times, more careful analysis may reveal the need for strengthening certain muscle groups or practicing breathing exercises to reduce stress if that's affecting performance.

The coach told him, "Repetition is the mother of learning. You will start loving the sport and the higher levels of challenge only if you are thorough with the fundamentals. You would have noticed the way I throw new challenges to juniors. If they are working on a straight drive and have become proficient, then I will challenge the skill by asking them to hit an on-drive through a 2m goal through mid-on. I don't make the challenge too tough, which will switch them off."

He continued, "Same with the bowling, hitting targets on a length, yorkers etc. 18-24 balls at a time. Don't be in a rush. You need to have as much fun as possible. You need to build the skills year after year."

34
New Delhi – 2 years later

Trisha came across an interesting article about the Prime Minister's Social Innovation Award. Social innovations, as the article explained are new strategies, concepts and ideas that meet the social needs of different elements which can be from working conditions and education to community development and health – they extend and strengthen the civil society.

She was reading it loud for Puneet to hear, "Social innovation includes the social processes of innovation – Innovations which have a social purpose – like activism, online volunteering, microcredit etc."

The article listed out the criteria to apply for the award. She felt that Puneet should apply for it.

Puneet was not in favour of applying for it as he felt if he deserves it, it will come in search of him.

He continued to focus on the projects. There are couple of projects in which he partnered with Ravinder and team. They had 100+ projects across 9 states in India, impacting more than 4000 villages. With 'water' at the core of everything that they do, lot of initiatives were undertaken with the aim of conserving water bodies in India.

"Let us introduce the concept of 'water budgeting' which involves 'Jal Sevaks' to ensure optimal, rightful and efficient consumption of water. These Jal Sevaks can lead the water conservation activities in their own and the adjoining 4-5 villages." Puneet told Shreya and his team.

Shreya said, "It's a great idea! They can also aim at motivating and enabling rural communities towards water harvesting and conservation."

With the help of local bodies, Puneet and team facilitated the construction of check dams and many other water harvesting structures to enable better drinking water and sanitation facilities at these villages.

Florida

Ekta was aware of the great things Puneet and his team were doing in India. She had a terrible guilt about the way Mike snatched the company from Puneet. She did not want her family to get impacted by the wrath so felt the need to do something for Puneet and his NGO. She reached out to Trisha and checked whether she can volunteer to mobilize some funds for their organization.

Ekta told Trisha, "I still feel very bad about the way things turned out. Not sure what Puneet feels about the entire stuff now. He might not be having good vibes for Mike and me."

Trisha replied, "Nothing like that. We have moved on. I don't think it bothers him anymore."

She continued, "There are lot of interesting things happening.

Puneet is very engrossed in some of the projects which he has taken up. Things are progressing well by the grace of God."

Ekta was happy to hear that. But she had planned a big donation to Puneet's NGO. Her only doubt was that whether he will accept it if it's coming from her even though Mike is not aware of it.

She planned to make that donation through her company in India. It was to the tune of USD 200,000.

Trisha told her that she will discuss with Puneet and get back to her.

Ekta had a strong reason to make this offer. Things were not going so well between Mike and her. When she discussed this matter with her father, he went to an astrologer. The astrologer mentioned about some ill feelings from someone who was close to Ekta as a reason for the trouble. He also said that along with certain rituals in the temples, she should do a financial help to this person who has been hurt badly because of the deeds of her husband. When her father told her about it, she could not think of anyone other than Puneet.

35

Paris, Annecy and Dijon

Rina wanted to spend some time with Abhinav as it was vacation time for him. She booked tickets for her parents and Abhinav. It was his second visit to Paris. Rajesh and Ruchita were travelling for the first time.

She planned to spend some quality time with them so took leave for few days.

They reached on Wednesday. 2 days later, they went to Annecy, a dreamy weekend getaway from Paris. Her boss recommended some places in Annecy, the Venice of France.

The way around the canals led to the most breathtaking lake – Lake Annecy.

Aside from that, the exciting thing was that they were near the Swiss border and the alps, meaning they have plenty of hearty alpine food to enjoy. Annecy is an amazing place like no other, making it one of the best weekend trips from Paris!

Rajesh became bit emotional. He was remembering the tough days they had to go through after Nilanjan's demise.

He told Rina, "I'm so proud of you, my girl. Many people can't even think of going through the things you have gone through in life. Inspite of all the hardships and setbacks, you made it big."

Rina had tears in her eyes. Abhinav held his mom closely.

Ruchita added, "She is an inspiration to lot of people in our family."

Rina said, "We all went through that phase together. I'm so blessed to have such a supporting family." She kissed her mom.

From Annecy they went to Dijon. One of Rina's clients had a beautiful mansion there and they were kind to offer for Rina to occupy their place during her visit; an offer that Rina found difficult to deny; it was a beautiful mansion even by the pictures. Dijon is an ultimate destination for food lovers. Not only is Dijon known for its food, but it is the capital of Burgundy and super close to some of the best vineyards in the world!

They explored the Les Halles Market and went for sampling some of the Burgundian specialties including mustard, crème de cassis and tarte tatin.

As Abhinav is a big fan of art and paintings, they went to Ducal Palace and Musee Des Beaux Arts Dijon. This museum was opened in 1787 and considered to be one of the oldest museums of France.

Rajesh and Abhinav walked around and admired the varied collection of art. They had a very good collection of Egyptian antiquities with a rare series of Fayum mummy portraits and some famous works from the Renaissance, dating back to the 17th and 18th centuries.

36

Rina had an opportunity to spend a lot of time with her parents and son after a long time. Work related commitments did not bother her so much.

Due to her intense travel for work, she gets to meet lot of people. During one of her visits to London she met Philip Winslet, the chef and owner of one of the famous French restaurants in London, Le Gascon. They were awarded Michelin Star in 2006 and they have retained it every year since.

London

Philip's maternal great-great-grandfather came to the UK from Sweden in 1890 as a tailor. Many people in his family took laboring jobs to make ends meet. His mother worked as nanny and a waitress. He and his siblings always had holidays out of the back of a van with a tent.

Rina met Philip during one of the high-profile fashion events in London. Philip and his team were responsible for the catering at the event.

She tasted some of their signature dishes and really loved it. She met Philip and showered lot of kind words about the food.

During the conversation, he found her very vibrant, smart and sweet.

He invited her to his restaurant, Le Gascon. She went for dinner next day and he treated her like a queen, laying out the best spread with a combo of French and Indian delicacies. She was floored. While leaving the restaurant, he hugged her and there was this utter peace that just swept over her. Her body was telling the brain what she already knew – He was the one.

2 days later, they met for coffee and talked for hours with amazing eye contact. She felt so comfortable with him, as if they had known each other for years. Soon after, their relationship took a romantic turn.

Rina was at a point in life where she was feeling bit lonely as her parents and son were away. She wanted to find a partner and settle down. She loved the way Philip made her feel so special.

She gave a hint about this relationship to her parents and Abhinav during their visit to Paris.

New Delhi

Prime Minister's Social Innovation Awards were declared. Puneet's 'Revive Lakes' project won the award for cleaning up more than 100 lakes across 9 states in India, impacting more than 4000 villages. The jury mentioned that the project demonstrated collaborative leadership and creative resilience to look at innovative solutions to reimagine our cities.

The jury appreciated Puneet Khosla for being a 'Futuremaker' by embracing the future with creative fearlessness and relentless purpose. They felt Puneet and team really focused on cultivating knowledge and community networks leading to collaborative action in a very effective manner.

Rajesh and Ruchita were so elated. They were always so proud of what their children achieved but this one was very special. Winning an award of this repute made them dance with joy!

Rajesh called Puneet, "Congratulations beta!!! So proud of you!!" He could not complete the sentence as the tears of joy rolled down.

Ruchita, Rina and Abhinav also joined the video call and wished Puneet for this amazing accomplishment.

37

New Delhi – 2 months later

Rajesh was going through the newspaper in the morning. He was so elated to see the news on the front page of Times of India.

The front page had the picture of Romil Singh's father, Ajay Singh, who walked out of Tihar prison in Delhi for two weeks. His statement read, "Today, I'm known in the public as Romil's father". A former MP, he said it was hard to believe that in just two years Romil has built the party and some of its candidates made even stalwarts bite the dust.

He kept reading.

Romil trounced CMP sitting MLA Deepti Sharma, wife of former Union Minister Kamlesh Sharma and many of his KRP party colleagues defeated senior ministers in 5 constituencies in the state.

The results of the Delhi Assembly elections possibly settled the debate on the legacy of former Union Home Minister and stalwart Ram Pratap Singh in the favour of his great grandson Romil Singh.

Hitting out at the KRP for its post-poll support to RJP, former Chief Minister and CMP leader Bhupinder Sisodia called it an "alliance of convenience".

On Sunday, RJP's Anil Mathur was sworn-in as the Chief Minister of Delhi after the party stitched a post-poll alliance with the KRP to form government in the state. KRP leader, Romil Singh took oath as the deputy Chief minister.

In the State Assembly elections, the ruling RJP fell short of a majority by winning a total of 41 seats of a 90-member House, the CMP and KRP came second and third with 35 and 12 seats respectively.

Romil emerged as the kingmaker, the support of whose party ensured a second term for the RJP.

Rajesh was so happy and called Romil and Nidhi. He wished them continued success and conveyed blessings from him and his wife.

Florida

Ekta gets to know that Mike was with Sarah for a week, and she gets really upset. She also noticed that Mike was losing interest in the business, and he was going off track. She knew that things are getting complicated.

Howard Smith and Anurag Saxena, Mike's partners in the real estate business were getting very aggressive and trying to get things under their hold. Ekta knew that Mike would not bother to get back and take things to the next level.

She spoke to Mike candidly about her worries, but he was in no mood to listen. Ekta could not believe that the things were exactly going the way the astrologer had predicted.

38

Mumbai Indians' training camp – One year later

Captain Sharma, Bumrah and Kishan were the latest to join the squad. Mumbai Indians set the ground running in preparation for the upcoming IPL campaign.

The 12-day strength and conditioning pre-season camp, ahead of Mumbai Indians' first match is being held at their in-house training facility at Reliance Jio Stadium in Navi Mumbai. They will also be playing a couple of inter-squad practice matches towards the second week of the camp.

Abhinav was bit nervous during the player assessment analysis by the coaching staff led by director of cricket Zaheer Khan and coach Mahela Jayawardene. But the selection team found him very good with the fundamentals.

Over the next 11 weeks, the coaching staff planned for the upskilling sessions for the young domestic and international recruits through individual sessions, game situations, mental aspects and physical fitness. Zaheer and Mahela were joined by

Shane Bond, Robin Singh, Kiran More, Rahul Sanghvi and data analyst CKM Dhananjai – who have a proven record of nurturing the likes of Suryakumar, Bumrah, Ishan, Pandya brothers and many more in the past.

Abhinav spoke to his grand dad, mom and uncle to share the excitement of training with some of the bigwigs in the field of cricket. He could not believe the pace at which things were happening in his life. He was grateful for everything. He knew his father's soul was guiding him.

Earlier, Captain Rohit Sharma accompanied by speedster Jasprit Bumrah moved from bubble to bubble to join the squad late last night, while Ishan Kishan flew from Bengaluru separately after securing full-fitness certificate from BCCI's NCA.

San Francisco

Howard and Anurag were investors in Puneet's venture, and they sought help from him to get his previous company back to track. They spoke to Mike and Ekta about their decision to move them from the board. The separation package was sweetened so that they don't mess up things.

Puneet was not keen to join them full time but offered to be a consultant. He had fantastic relationships with the key clients and had a good understanding of the platforms which catered to clients in different sectors.

Mike and Ekta only focused on the clients from real estate sector, and this was the prime reason for the downfall in all other sectors. Howard and Anurag had full faith in Puneet and knew that he can help them to revive the company. They sent him the contract offering him USD 500,000 for the first year to get things right.

Puneet was really amazed with the way things were falling into his lap.

He spent first few weeks in New York and SFO meeting the technology teams. Many of the team members were very happy to see him at the helm again. The meetings also helped him to understand some of the issues with the legacy platforms. Few days later, he started meeting his old clients and many of them showed willingness to associate with him.

He knew the second innings is going to be far brighter and more blessed than the first one!